Zanchier

Book 2

Uprising

SG Boudreaux

SG BOUDREAUX

BOOK 2 OF THE ZANCHIER SERIES

UPRISING

ISBN: 978-1-7361117-3-4 (Paperback)

ISBN: 978-1-7361117-2-7 (Digital)

All rights reserved. No part of this publication may be reproduced, or transmitted in any form or by any means, including photocopying, recording, or other electronic or mechanical methods without the prior written permission of the publisher. For permission requests, solicit the publisher via the email address below.

SG Boudreaux

PO Box 12936

Lake Charles, La. 70612

Printed in the USA

Sgboodro2@yahoo.com

www.SGBoudreaux.com

Copyright © year 2021 by SG Boudreaux

All rights reserved

Glossary

Section with all CAPPED letters is the annunciated part of the word having inflection. Bold letters receive the long sound.

Praxtingen (PRAX tin jin)	Mid-size city eastern territory
Loradin (LOR a dun)	Large island city eastern territory.
Martanzia (Mar TAN zee u)	Large city, northern territory
Bakrashan (Ba kru Shan)	Large city, western territory
Carpasmere (Car PA smear)	Mid-sized city, north-eastern territory, mostly housing based.
Kabihanxu (Ka BI han jew)	A massively large, four-legged, fire-breathing, bird whose feathers are streaked in shades of red, yellow, orange, purple, teal, and gold. Its skin is like armor. Carnivorous. Slang term is **Firebird.**
Monshokto (Mon SHOCK toe)	A large, furry, long-haired creature, with a single horn in the middle of its head. Runs on all fours but walks on two legs. Eats fish and grass.
Trefell (Tre FELL)	Smallish to medium sized ball of fur with sharp teeth. They can roll along at quicker speeds. Downs trees.
*Tribhon (**TRI** bun)*	Cross between a squirrel and racoon with a stinging tail and long, sharp retractable claws. Eats fruit and nuts.
*Raisedback Vindaper (**RAI**SED back VIN du pair)*	Resembles a wild boar. Eats mushrooms, and scraps.

*Yarequu (Yar **A** koo)*	Resembles a very large horse. Eats fruits, berries, nuts, grasses.
Pagorinx (PA gor inx)	A massive, cat-like creature whose fur is so black It's almost purple. It has teal and white braided looking stripes from its ears to its rear haunches, sharp retractable claws-teal in color. Long, braided looking hair around its neck, long sabered teeth that protrude from the top lip. Carnivorous.
*Zanch**ieth** (Zan **KEETH**)*	Wealthiest people, Old world money.
*Rh**e** Mines (R**ay**)*	Mines with minerals known as Rhenium and Ruthenium. Highly sought after for their high melting point. And used in weapons and armor against the Kabihanxu.
*Scaithers (**SKA** thers)*	Ruthless, lawless, band of people.
*Rhedon (**Ray** dawn)*	Zanchier's monetary system.

For a detailed view of the map, sign up for my email list via my website; listed in the back of the book; on the contact me page. As an email subscriber, you can sign up to get free members only access to book-related content for all my books.

Table of Contents

Chapter 1	Praxtingen	1
Chapter 2	Bain's Decision	9
Chapter 3	Seadon and FAZ	17
Chapter 4	Wynne's Gift	25
Chapter 5	Gracelynn's Haunted Dreams	33
Chapter 6	Hard Decisions	43
Chapter 7	Harper's Intuition	53
Chapter 8	The Bounty	61
Chapter 9	On Their Own	69
Chapter 10	LSS Resistance	75
Chapter 11	Breached Borders	85
Chapter 12	Misunderstood	93
Chapter 13	Wars and Rumors of War	101
Chapter 14	A Country Divided	109
Chapter 15	Preparing For War	123
Chapter 16	Choosing Sides	129
Chapter 17	And So It Begins	137
Chapter 18	Reactions and Consequences	145
Chapter 19	Who's Fighting Who?	153
Chapter 20	Into Hiding	163
Chapter 21	A Small Victory	173
Chapter 22	An Uncertain Future	185
	About the Author	193
	Other Books by SG Boudreaux	194

Chapter 1

Praxtingen

Sixteen-year-old Bain Brinley rode the public transport module through the massive gates of Loradin and out across the glass skybridge. The bridge somehow seemed to float over Everly Lake, linking the island of Loradin to the mainland. He loved going over the bridge into Praxtingen. His father, Wilkins Brinley, grew up there, and for a smaller town on the edge of Loradin it had its perks. Just being able to move to Loradin was hard enough, and he had yet to make any real friends. Of course, making friends wasn't the most important thing right now. He was finally sixteen, graduated from academy, and ready to find his own place. He just wasn't sure if he wanted to live in Loradin or Praxtingen. He liked the feel of the smaller city, and he wouldn't be far from his work in Loradin. His grandfather, Aaric Brinley, was head of the Loradin Secret Service. His alias was Uncle, which was what all the agents called him. Since Bain was family, he could take a position in the LSS, but he had wanted to earn it on his own. Bain was extremely smart and good with technology which had allowed him to test well for a position in the company.

He had recently also been in contact with his best friend from Port Proud, Kreelie Rintel, trying to get Kreelie to apply to the LSS. Kreelie was a prime candidate as well for the LSS since he was at the Port Proud Academy for the Technically Advanced and Gifted. Kreelie's specialty was motors. He could take apart any engine and put it back together without the aid of a manual. He had a photographic memory which enabled his ability, and which helped him through academy. Bain really hoped that Kreelie chose to mentor here at the LSS. Bain had really missed his best friend over the last four months.

Since moving to Loradin, he had run into a few people he used to see roaming the halls at academy. Back then, they had been Loradians, and what was the point of making friends with people you'd never see again except at academy. He had never expected to move here. No one just moved to Loradin because of the difficulty to get approval to enter the city. The Loradian government was very strict about who they let in. The only way his family had easily gotten in was because his grandfather was leader of the LSS and had their papers cleared long before he knew what was happening. His parents, who had been missing themselves for years due to the Zanchier government's forced service programs, had just shown up one day at his grandparent's house, loaded them all up on an airship -including Grandmother Gracelynn- and the next thing he knew, they were in Loradin at his father's parent's house, whom he barely remembered from lack of contact over the years.

The public transport module slowed to a stop at the street corner near Praxtingen Market. The market was bustling with activity this morning. It was open every day, allowing local and non-local artisans to sell their wares. Farmers, small-time miners with their handmade trinkets, painters, jewelers, writers, sculptors, module parts, food vendors, you name it, the market had it. Yarequu, used to pull carts and wagons to market, were tied up at the end near the make-shift barn area, which in reality was an old, abandoned, building from years back that the city decided to turn into animal housing for the market. It housed many other types of live animals that were for sale at the market, including those for butchering.

Bain was often drawn to the barn. He loved looking at the massive Yarequu, and often marveled at how gentle they could be. Their long manes and tails streaked white and teal against their grayish and blue pelts. The spikes that protruded from their knee joints on all four legs made him wonder what their purpose was. Their heads were triangular in shape with a hard looking plate that sat in the middle of their heads, stretched out to their eyes and down their nose. This particular Yarequu was large, but he had seen larger over the years. He had heard tale of some as big as twenty hands high and eight hands wide at the chest. Many of the animals of Zanchier were shrouded in mystery. Some were used to help around farms and in other areas. But Bain had seen so many creatures over the last year that he had never before noticed. Like the Monshokto that lived on the banks of Everly Lake. The large hairy, one-horned creatures were grouped along the shoreline in the different areas. They lived in pods and could be seen in small groups, curled up like rocks on the shoreline. They could also be seen hunting for fish as they swam happily in the lake. The biggest pod he had witnessed so far consisted of seven Monshokto.

Wynne often came home from academy and talked about learning about the animals of Zanchier. They learned some about them in the academy back in Port Proud, but not like they did here in Loradin. Not only did they learn about them in detail, but here some of the animals were often used in an array of areas due to the animal rehabilitation facility on the outskirts of the city near the water. Injured creatures were often brought there for rehabilitation and returned to the wild. Because of this facility, the Loradians learned a great deal about all the creatures of Zanchier.

Some activity caught Bain's attention at the other side of the market. One of the animal vendors was struggling with a Raisedback Vindaper. The animal was nearly thigh high, with short hair, which was brownish black in color, with a large spike of hair that ran from his shoulders to his tail, decreasing in height near the haunches. It had three sets of tusks on its face. One that protruded from the bottom of its jawline at the back of the head and curved forward. The other two sets stuck upward from its mouth at the rear of the jaw. It had three legs on each side, a longish, whiplike tail, and was mean tempered. It had little fear of anything in the wild. The tamed ones they bred for meat were better tempered, but you still had to be careful around them, as displayed by the vendor at the moment. Apparently the animal didn't want to go into the pen and was causing quite a ruckus. Bain watched in humor when his attention was suddenly drawn upward and off to the side at a few girls who were watching him and waving.

Bain quickly straightened his posture, nodded politely, and turned to walk away. He noticed that girls sometimes watched him. It made him self-conscious, like he had something on his face, or his hair was a mess. His mother Harper told him it was because he was a good-looking young man just like his father Wilkins had been at his age. Bain wasn't interested in any of these girls though. He had one particular girl on his mind, and he had met her purely by accident one day while exploring Loradin.

Raila Orman worked at the Loradin Animal Rehabilitation Sanctuary, often referred to as the LARS institute. He had noticed animals wondering around the banks of Everly Lake in fenced areas and decided to go inside and ask questions. He soon made friends with several of the employees. Nowhere else in Zanchier did they have such a place as the LARS Institute.

"Bain!" someone yelled.

Bain was shaken from his thoughts at the sound of his name being called across the market. He looked up to see Silus, one of the market vendors who had befriended Bain on his first visit there three months back.

"Hey Silus." Bain waved to the older man as he walked across the street. Silus was in his forties, slightly balding, tall, thick, and strong. Bain walked over to his friend's booth as Silus threw a large piece of smoked meat from a cooling-box onto the table for a customer. Bain waited for him to finish with the customer, and his friend soon turned his attention toward Bain.

"Good morning, Bain. What are you doing over in these parts today?"

Bain smiled at his friend. He never beat around the bush.

"Just felt like exploring some more today since it's my day off."

"You come to the market quite often. Wouldn't you like to explore somewhere else for a change?"

"I do. I go out most every evening after work. I just like the energy in the marketplace."

"Fair enough. But, if you get a chance, you might want to go up into the Carpasian Mountains a bit. There are some mighty beautiful spots up that way. The waterfalls are extraordinary."

"Thanks, Silus. I'll keep that in mind."

Silus handed Bain a slice of the smoked meat.

"Thanks, Silus."

"Not a problem. Gotta' keep you growing boys strong." Silus smiled and winked at Bain. "You go on now and see what you can get into. But stay out of trouble." Silus grinned.

"Me? Get into trouble?" Bain feigned innocence. He smiled and waved to Silus, munching the savory smoked meat as he wondered away to explore the morning's offerings at the market. As Bain walked along viewing the wares for sale, his mind took him to the decisions he would have to soon make.

Back in Martanzia, when prospects graduated the academy, they were placed into housing befitting their stations and their talents. This was where they would spend the next year mentoring in the workforce. Then they were moved into housing according to their job's location. If things went very well for them, they could eventually move into better housing but within the same complex.

Here in Loradin, things were a little different. Bain got to select where he wanted to live. Either in the inner city of Loradin, or in one of the outlying towns like Praxtingen. Maybe that was just because of the field he chose to enter into? Being an agent or employee of the LSS was different than most jobs. The agents worked wherever they were sent. However, Bain wasn't going to be an agent. He was going to work in the technical labs helping to build new technology for the LSS agents and Loradin. He just wasn't sure that was where he wanted to be. Bain had always leaned toward electronics, but the older he got, and with the recent developments concerning his grandfather's imprisonment and the evil that the LSS had uncovered, he felt like he wanted to be out there doing something more, not stuck inside a building creating things for others to use. He wondered if he would be allowed to switch his career if it wasn't based on his talent? He knew that if he were anywhere else in Zanchier other than Loradin, that question would receive a steadfast no. But here in Loradin, he just might be able to do so. Bain smiled at the future he imagined for himself. He would ask his grandfather this evening if switching his career direction were something he could do.

Deciding where to live was another problem. In Martanzia he sort of lived on the outskirts of the city. Everly Sound had been a quiet coastal community, but it was for Zanchieths only. His grandparents had been Zanchieths, so he supposed that sort of made him and his siblings Zanchieth as well. But Bain considered himself Praxer, like his parents had been.

In Zanchier, their social statuses were defined by their class rankings. The Zanchieths were the upper crust of society, and the rules apparently did not apply to them. The Praxers were the next level. Self-made men and women who made their own fortunes by the sweat of their brows. Then, there were the Carpasians and Bakrisians. This group made up the majority of Zanchier's population and were the poorest of all. They were often abused by the Zanchieths and sent to work the harvest fields or the Rhe mines, which didn't amount to much rhedon, what measly amount was left of their earnings went for food, rent on the horrid homes provided, and other necessities. The Zanchieths owned most of the property in the outlying towns and charged large amounts of rhedon for dilapidated living quarters. The last social group was the self-proclaimed Scaithers, and this group of people were the worst sort imaginable. They fancied themselves on the same level as the Zanchieths, above taxation and the law. The only difference was that the Scaithers were brutal, and they didn't care who saw it. They were taking over Zanchier quickly, and Bain's grandfather and the LSS were ever watchful and working to stop them. The Scaithers, however, had their claws locked into a lot of the Zanchieths. They had some very powerful people backing them, and the LSS feared they would soon control the military forces outside of Loradin's reach.

Bain's own family had been torn apart by that very same organization. When his father was forced into military service, it was by the government. Then the Scaithers appeared as a false resistance, basically pretending to fight themselves; and that was when they had kidnapped his mother. His grandparents had thought that the government had taken Harper, but it had been under the control of one Commander Raif Martray. The man was the leader of the Scaithers and apparently had control over many of the government leaders of Zanchier, all except for the Loradian government. His reach didn't extend this far, and Bain hoped it never would. But he knew that the LSS and his grandfather worried about his power and fought hard to keep Raif Martray's influence out of Loradin.

Bain shook the heavy thinking from his mind and got back to thinking about where he wanted to live. In the bustling inner city and protective walls of Loradin, or a quieter, country-type life like back on Everly Sound? One person might influence his decision. If he lived in Loradin, then he would be able to visit Raila Orman more often. But if he lived in Praxtingen he would be able to explore the countryside easier. He could visit Raila after work before he left for home since he would be working in the city anyway. Bain smiled. He would have to think on this a while apparently. If he moved to Praxtingen, he maybe could find a small place on the fringe of the smaller city with a view of Everly Lake, maybe by next week. He would also see if his old friend Kreelie had decided yet about applying to the LSS. If he did, and got the job, they could rent a place together.

Bain's future looked brighter than it ever had before. He took a deep breath of the fresh, country air, walked the market for a bit longer, and decided to see about renting a mod or a Yarequu to ride out to the Carpasian Mountains to see about finding a few of those waterfalls Silus had spoken about earlier. Of course, his mother warned him about straying too far from civilization because of Raif Martray, but his grandfather had told him that Raif had no control near Loradin, and frankly, Bain was tired of worrying about the man or looking over his shoulder. His mother did enough of that for all of them. He wouldn't live his life that way. No, here in Loradin he felt more free than ever before, and he planned to take full advantage of it in every way possible. Bain found a small mod for rent, hopped in, and took off for the base of the Carpasian Mountains looking for adventure.

SG Boudreaux

Chapter 2

Bain's Decision

Bain rode across the unpaved roads that ran toward the Carpasian Mountains. He could see one of the waterfalls in the distance that Silus had mentioned. It fell from the top of the mountainside down toward the valley below. As Bain got closer the details of the large falls began to take shape.

Bain found a spot to park the Mod and climbed out. This was the first waterfall he had ever seen up close. He stood in amazement for a little while, marveling over the expanse of it. As children, they had never been allowed to wander too close to the mountain base for fear of the large predatory animals; his memories reminding him to keep his wits about him.

The waterfall started its cascade at about a hundred feet up, twisting and turning its way through and over rocks that jutted out at different spots along the water's path. It looked to be about thirty-feet wide at the top and stretched and split around rocks at the base to around fifty feet where it filled a wide but small basin. The basin had about three small streams that branched out in different directions, running into the forest on either side, and out over a lush valley straight ahead. He noticed that the summer flowers had mostly waned, and the heat was starting to wilt what was left, as the hottest part of summer would soon be over, and fall would be ushered in on the mountain winds as they briskly blew across the lake.

Bain stood basking in the overspray of the falls as it pounded the basin in front of him. The water cooled his skin and made it tingle as the mist hit his flesh. He stripped off his shoes and most of his clothing, making sure to take off anything that might sparkle in the sunlight, and dove into the cool welcoming water. It wasn't deep along the edges. He could easily stand in most of the sandy, rocky, bottom of the basin. He swam over to the waterfall, keeping an eye out for glowfish, especially Stingers. They were the ones with the stinging tentacles they had always been warned about in academy. Those fish were attracted to sparkly things and often killed with one stinging touch, making for a long, miserable, and painful death. Stingers were mostly found at Lumen Falls and in certain places around Everly Lake where the tributaries from those falls emptied into it.

Bain swam up underneath the waterfall and stood beneath the lighter cascading areas of water. He climbed up the rocks that sat beneath the falls and explored behind the falling water. Near the center of the falls was a section of rock that sat back further than the sides. He walked back toward the rock facing and discovered a cavern back inside the mountain, peering inside the opening but unable to see much further past the entry for lack of daylight. He sensed that the cavern was fairly large but would have to come back later with a light to explore better. Maybe he would even bring Seadon and Wynne with him?

"Seadon would really get a kick out of this," Bain said out loud.

He turned back to the waterfall behind him and dove in, enjoying the swim and exploring for the next half-hour before climbing out, drying off a bit, and then climbing back inside his Mod to explore a bit more of the small, winding, seemingly forgotten, dirt road that climbed up into the mountains. He traveled for half a mile before the road disappeared completely amongst the thick trees. Bain was curious why the road would suddenly just vanish. There was no destination, only a thick forest that loomed in front of him.

He decided to call it a day, not wishing to find himself in any trouble going on alone. Besides, his stomach was growling something fierce, and he hadn't thought to bring a lunch. He turned the Mod toward Praxtingen and drove the twenty or so miles back to town and the market square to grab lunch.

Perhaps Silus is still there, and we can chat about what I found? Silus probably knows about the waterfall and cave. Maybe he can tell me about it, Bain thought.

Zanchier Book 2: Uprising

As Bain drove toward the market, he thought some more about where he would choose to live. He could easily explore like this all the time if he lived in or around Praxtingen. But, if he chose Loradin City, he could be near Raila. He liked Raila a lot, but was it enough to base a decision about where to live? Then there was his commitment to take Wynne to LARS every Friday. Living in the city would make all of that easier, and he would be closer to work. Even if it were only by fifteen minutes. Bain decided that living in the city would be best, but he could come explore the outer rims of the towns anytime he wanted, and he could easily bring his siblings with him. Now he had to find an apartment. He decided to spend the remainder of the afternoon searching Loradin for a place where he might like to live.

Bain smiled to himself. He was happy and ready to make his own life decisions. He thought about how his entire family had been reunited and everyone was doing well. Soon he would be completely independent, have his own place, and a job he really enjoyed with the option of becoming an LSS agent. And maybe he could even talk Kreelie into rooming with him and applying to the LSS. After all that, the next step would be convincing Raila Orman to go on a date with him.

The edges of Praxtingen city and the town market were in sight. Minutes later, Bain drove the Mod back to the rental station then went to see Silus and maybe have lunch with the burly man. What he didn't notice was the attention he had captured.

Castor Briggs sat at one of the open-air tables of the market with a Palm-Cast, projecting onto a thin, small, glass screen that slid up above the device to project whatever data the user wished to view. Cass, as most called him, watched Bain Brinley, matching the young man with the data on the screen of the Palm-Cast. Every bounty hunter in Zanchier was looking for the Brinleys. He would collect a large payday for bringing just one in. But if he could catch Harper Brinley, he'd be set for life. Word on the line was she stole something very valuable from Raif Martray, and he was willing to pay handsomely to get it back. Luckily, Cass had just found his first clue as to where the Brinleys might be staying. Cass wasn't certain where they were living, but he could certainly entice Harper Brinley out of hiding by snatching one of her kids. He sat calmly drinking the cool liquid and forming a plan in his mind as he scanned the market crowds for other would-be bounty hunters. He planned on collecting on this one, and he didn't favor sharing his find with anyone else. His attention returned to young Bain Brinley and the man called Silus.

Silus smiled at the young man approaching. "Hey, Bain. Where have you been off to this morning?"

"I took your advice and headed out toward the Carpasian Mountains and a waterfall."

"Did you find the large one just off the main road?"

"Sure did. It's really beautiful out there. I also found a cave behind the waterfall. Did you know it was there?" Bain asked, taking a seat with Silus, and handing him one of the two large sandwiches he had purchased for himself and his friend.

"Thanks, Bain." Silus held up the sandwich. "Yeah, I know about that waterfall. The cavern inside is pretty large too. It also holds a few interesting secrets. Keep that in mind when you go exploring again." Silus grinned mischievously at Bain.

"What! You mean you're just going to leave me in suspense and not tell me?"

Silus laughed. "What would be the fun in that? You need to find out for yourself."

"True," Bain stated, smiling at the man beside him. "I bet you were trouble when you were my age."

"What kind of boy would I have been if I weren't?" Silus winked at Bain as they both laughed and chatted for the next thirty minutes while they ate their lunch.

The city transport Module was due to return any second, and Bain needed to catch it for a ride back into Loradin. He bid farewell to Silus and made it to the stop just in time to board the public Mod.

Cass Briggs watched as the public Mod made its way toward Loradin.

Hmm, Loradin, Briggs thought. He would have to see if he could find a way into Loradin. But surely Bain Brinley would make another appearance here at the Praxtingen Market soon enough. He would just have to wait and watch, and maybe even chat up the man called Silus for some information on the Brinleys.

That was the thing about being a bounty hunter, to be a good one you had to learn patience. Manipulation was also a great tool if you learned to use it well, and Castor Briggs was a pro. He had to learn to survive at an early age. And not only did he survive, but he often thrived. Most called him cruel and heartless. Cass just preferred to call it looking out for number one. He had learned that kindness and feelings only got you burned and left you hungry. He learned to never let feelings get in his way, and it had served him well. Cass finished his beverage and went to rent a room overlooking the market. He'd bide his time and wait for Bain's return. Then, he'd make his move. He could barter the boy for Harper, and, if he got lucky enough, maybe he could make it a family occasion. He could retire off this hunt if he played his cards right.

Bain rode the Mod back into Loradin, taking his leave at the LSS headquarters. He would first talk to his grandfather about recruiting Kreelie, then possibly about changing his job placement. Then he would talk to Kreelie about moving here. He made his way to the tech floor, let Maubrey know he was taking one of the new Bi-Mods, the newly developed two-wheeled modules based off of Uncle Finn's homemade Voyager, and took off to explore the cities offerings for apartments. Maybe he could find something really close to LARS. Having a view of the water would be nice. Working for the LSS in the tech department got him a pretty decent paycheck. He could afford something a bit nicer than the normal graduation starter place graduates were often given. Another plus was that he wouldn't have to live in a community with the same people with which he had attended academy. He drove around the city looking at any and all promising places, stopping to go inside and inquire of any openings for rent. He found one place in particular that was a third-floor, corner apartment and only a few blocks from LARS. It had a spectacular view of Everly Lake, and he could see almost all of the Loradin Animal Rehabilitation Sanctuary.

Bain turned to the building manager. "I'll take it."

The woman pursed her lips and looked Bain over. "You seem awful young ta' be able ta' afford this place."

"Don't worry. You'll get your money."

"Shouldn't you be in a training community?"

"Look, if you don't want my money I'm sure I can find another place that will." Bain began to walk through the door.

"All right!" The suspicious woman stated. "The place is yours. First month and deposit due upon signing. And no wild parties or you'll be out on your rear-end faster than you can blink."

Bain smiled widely and shook the woman's hand. "Great. I'll be back this evening to move in."

They went downstairs to sign the contract and Bain used his new wrist scanner to pay what was due.

The building manager looked at him, curious how one so young would be in a position to pay with a wrist scanner. Most of the established professionals of high-end jobs were apparently the only people to have such a device, but she shrugged it off, happy to have rented the place.

Bain was smiling broadly as he exited Bayview Apartments. He felt like a real adult. His grandfather Aaric had given him the wrist scanner on his first day at the LSS. His paycheck was automatically deposited every week. Most places, like the Praxtingen market didn't have the technology to take payment by wrist scanner so he always carried some rhedon with him. But for larger purchases, it sure made it much easier.

Now he had to go home and tell his mother that he was moving out. He knew she was expecting it, but they had only just been reunited for the last four months. He knew she was going to worry. And, if he were truly honest, she had every right to. His parents, especially his mother, had been through a living hell for five years. There were things that

Zanchier Book 2: Uprising

she still wouldn't tell him and his siblings. He could understand not telling Seadon and Wynne, but he was an adult now and could handle the truth, but he wouldn't push her about her past. He knew she often still had nightmares. He could hear her yelling in the night, and his father trying to calm her down. She did say once that the nightmares didn't really start until after it was all over. Her body just couldn't relax and let go of the past. It haunted her most nights, and very seldom lately did she sleep well. His mother was the strongest person he knew. Not even his father Wilkins, who had been forced into the military by the Zanchier government; which they all knew now as the Scaither organization; had experienced half of what his mother had.

Bain drove the Bi-Mod through the Loradin streets headed for home just fifteen minutes across town. He would spend the rest of the afternoon packing, and then have a talk with his family when everyone got home. He wanted to make tonight his first night in his new apartment. He was so excited about his future that he pulled over to the side of the road overlooking the South Loradin Bay Beach and com-called Kreelie.

"Bain, buddy, what's up?" Kreelie's exuberant voice smiled at him from the other end.

"Kreelie, man, I just wanted to let you know what's happening here, see how things are there, and ask if you've decided yet about moving to Loradin with me?"

"Things are the same here. Lots of military movement on the ground. There are some thugs who seem to be terrorizing the outer territories. Dad's been dealing with a lot of complaints from the governors of the smaller villages about rebels coming around demanding protection money from all the business owners."

"That's rough. Does your dad know who these rebels are?"

"Scaithers I think. My dad says they are quickly growing in numbers, and it isn't the good kind. These men, and women, are a cruel bunch."

"Well, you can get away from all of that and come live with me here. I just got my own place today."

Kreelie was quiet for a minute. "That's great news Bain. But I'm still not sure what I'm going to do. I feel like I need to stay here, you know. Help the people *here* deal with these thugs. Dad got me on with the Policing Authority where he works. He *is* captain of the department after all."

"We do a lot of good with the LSS too, Kreelie. I really think you'd like it here."

"I don't know, Bain, maybe. Look, it's been good talking with you, but I have to get going. I have to report to the station super early for my first day tomorrow, and I have a lot to get ready, and get a good night's sleep."

"All right, Kreelie. Call me soon with your decision. I miss you, friend."

"I miss you too, Bain. Hey, enjoy your new apartment."

Bain could hear the smile in Kreelie's voice as they ended the call. But he also knew that Kreelie was keeping something from him. He worried that he and Kreelie were growing apart. The last thing Bain wanted was to lose his best friend.

Chapter 3

Seadon and FAZ

Seadon Brinley had been in FAZ; Future Airmen of Zanchier Training Program; for the last five years of his life. Leaving Martanzia, Port Proud, and the Martanzia Air Academy, had been a real bummer four months back, even though he had his parents back and had met his grandparents on his father's side of the family. Living in Loradin was definitely different, and he did get to train on an actual airship with an actual captain, but he missed FAZ classes back home and his friends. At the Martanzia Air Academy he had learned all about airships all day long, even though they hadn't perfected getting them to fly yet.

The Loradin FAZ Academy was different. He figured that they would learn more since the city already had an actual working airship. But they tended to focus on other things. Training with Captain Matt Easton was a twice a week thing and only for a few hours, and he had yet to get to steer an airship. The Captain was instructing him on all the instruments needed to fly the ship. He was also teaching him necessary maneuvers should they encounter a Kabihanxu. Not many Kabihanxu flew near the city of Loradin, or any other cities for that matter. They usually stayed near the mountains and valley towns to hunt. Captain Matt said that flying over the lake was unnecessary for their survival and only took them closer to man, their greatest adversary. Captain Matt had seen very few in all his years of test flights but did have an encounter with one or two during those few sightings. Tales of adventures he had promised to tell Seadon about at a later date.

The FAZ classes conducted here in Loradin consisted of other subjects as well. He had to take animal behavior classes, which was a surprise. He had no clue as to why he needed to know about a bunch of creatures he would likely never encounter. What was the purpose of knowing the habitats of the Monshokto, or the hidden abilities of the Yarequu, or why the Trefell chews down certain trees more often than other types? Seadon sighed heavily. All this other stuff was a waste of time, time he could be devoting to learning about flying.

He dragged himself off the academy transport Mod and across the lawn to his house. Today was not an airship day so he had little to occupy himself with, other than going over study material on Zanchier wildlife.

Wynne noticed her brother's long face.

"Hey Seadon. What's wrong with you today?"

"Just realizing I'm wasting my life away."

Wynne giggled at her overly dramatic brother. "What do you mean by that?"

"The FAZ classes here are different than back home."

"Everything is different here, Seadon. Not just your academy classes."

"I know. Most of it is good, but I feel like I'm not learning *anything* at academy."

"Then speak to mother and father. Maybe they'll have an answer."

Wynne skipped ahead of Seadon as he watched her go into the house, yelling hello to their mother.

"When did she get so smart?" Seadon said out loud to himself.

Wynne wasn't the only person to notice Seadon's defeated posture.

Harper watched her son drag his backpack across the floor and deposit it against the wall of the kitchen. He then drug himself to the cooler, grabbed a beverage, and plopped down on a tall stool at the bar. As he drank from the container, Harper watched him. When he stopped to take a breath, she asked him a question.

"Seadon, what's wrong?"

Seadon looked at his mother over the top of his beverage as he turned it up to take another long drink. He finally sat the container on the counter.

"Academy is boring."

"I thought you loved academy?" Harper asked, shocked.

"I did back in Port Proud, but here it's different. They make you learn all sorts of things I'll never need or use."

"I think your instructors know what you might need," Harper stated.

"I am never going to need to know about animals and their behaviors, habitats, and skills. How could that information possibly help me with flying?"

Harper, trying to hide the grin at her son's cocky overly stunned face and rolling eyes, replied. "Well, maybe they know something you don't. Like, I learned a lot about Kabihanxus and Pagorinxes while I was wondering through the Xantifal Mountains all those months ago. I learned things that could save my life and did on several occasions."

"That's different. You learned out of necessity. What do I need to know that stuff for?"

"Well, Seadon, I didn't think I would ever need to know all the things I've learned either. And the difference is I had to learn the hard way. Let's say you're flying over one of the mountain ranges one day and your airship crashes. You're trapped in the mountains for a time, and you have to survive on your own. Wouldn't it be nice to know a few things about the creatures that now surround you and have you at a big disadvantage?"

Seadon thought about what she said for a minute. "I suppose it would be beneficial in that scenario. But I doubt that will ever happen."

"I too doubted I would ever need to know how to fight or use a weapon. It's always good to have knowledge, even if you think you'll never need it."

"But I really do need more of a challenge, Mother. Academy is so easy. I feel like my talents are being wasted."

"All right, when your father gets home we'll discuss this further and see what we can come up with. But until then you need to apply yourself to learning whatever it is they want you to."

"Okay, okay, I get what you're saying."

Harper smiled at her thirteen-year-old, ruffled his hair, and kissed him on the head. "Good. Now go put your backpack away and take care of any *boring homework* before dinner, which is in an hour."

"Yes ma'am," Seadon said, saluting her as he turned, grabbed his pack, and slowly climbed the stairs.

Harper smiled, loving the daily interaction with her children. She hoped it would be years before any of them decided it was time to leave home. Seadon and Wynne still had several years in academy, but Bain had already graduated a few months back. They had a great celebration which also had included his sixteenth birthday party as well. He would have been put in a group community back in Martanzia, but here, he still lived at home. And Harper hoped that would continue at least a few more years, especially since they had all just found one another again after a five-year separation. Just as her thoughts concluded, she heard Bain arrive home on the new two wheeled Mods the LSS just created.

Bain walked in the kitchen with a smile as big as ever plastered across his face.

"Hi Mother." He walked over and kissed her on the cheek.

"Hi, Bain," she said, smiling. "You're in an awfully good mood."

"I'll tell you about it after dinner." Bain grabbed a drink from the cooler and took a long swig of the cold liquid.

"Where's Adda?" he asked, looking around for his youngest sister.

"She is spending the day with both grandmothers. Mother and Neitha took her shopping and who knows where else. Neitha wanted to keep her overnight."

"Good, that will free you up to listen at dinner." He smiled and took the stairs two at a time up to his room.

Harper yelled after him, "Dinner's in an hour!"

The house was quiet again as she went about finishing dinner and cleaning the kitchen, not wanting to spend any more time in the kitchen than necessary. She wanted to spend some quality time with her family after dinner instead of cleaning.

An hour later Wilkins walked into the house as Harper was putting dinner on the outside table. Everyone met on the patio where they chatted about everything they had done that day. Harper getting a bit agitated with Bain for going off on his own to explore.

"Bain, how many times must I tell you to be careful? It isn't safe to just take off by yourself like that and not let anyone know where you're going," Harper chided him.

"Mother, I'm sixteen. I can handle myself. Besides, I refuse to live in fear all the time. I understand what you went through, but I can't live like you do, always fearful."

"I just wish you could understand how evil Raif Martray is, and that he will stop at nothing to enact revenge."

"I'm sure the man has other things to occupy his time instead of looking for you just to get even."

Harper's blood began to boil. Wilkins placed his hand on hers to calm her down. He looked at Bain.

"Son, your Mother is right. Raif Martray is evil incarnate. I know what the man is capable of. And listen when we tell you, he doesn't take being bested with ease. Your mother destroyed all of his plans, along with the machine he spent years and rhedon building. Just please be careful and watchful when you go outside the Loradin walls, all right?"

"Yes sir, I promise. You and Mother won't have to worry about me for much longer anyway because I have some news," he beamed. "I rented an apartment today over near LARS and I plan on spending my first night there tonight."

Harper's breath caught in her throat, and she and Wilkins exchanged looks.

"I didn't know you were already looking, Bain." Harper looked down at her folded hands in her lap.

"I know you wanted us all to stay together longer, Mother. But I can't put my life on hold. I was supposed to go into community housing last month anyway. I'm just ready to get on with the next step in my life, especially now that things are so different than they would have been in Martanzia."

Harper sighed heavily. "I understand."

Bain squirmed at the pained looked on his Mother's face. "It's not like you'll never see me again. I'm only fifteen minutes away, and I still plan on taking Wynne to LARS every week. Plus, we work in the same building several days a week."

Harper grinned at her son's words. "You're right. As much as I would like to keep you all here forever, I know I can't do that."

Wilkins put in, "So, you need some help moving into this apartment of yours?"

"Sure. Besides, you all need to come see where I live anyway." Bain smiled broadly as they all excitedly chatted about his new place and the adult plans he was making. Harper joined in the conversation as much as possible, her stomach all jittery over the concept of her oldest moving out, and the chances he was taking with his safety. At least he had chosen to live inside the city gates of Loradin where his safety wouldn't be in question. But knowing that he went outside to Praxtingen made her worry. She knew he liked it and had friends there, but she also knew that Martray's reach could extend into the unprotected outer cities.

They cleaned up the dinner dishes, loaded all of Bain's stuff into Wilkins' and Harper's vehicles and left for Bain's new place. They put what little he had in the apartment and decided he needed a few more furniture pieces. They went back to the house and took his bed, dresser, and a few extra pieces of living room furniture over for him to have a place to sit until he could get his own furniture.

Wynne pointed out the apartment window, excitedly showing Harper and Wilkins the LARS building only a few blocks away where Bain took her every Friday evening. She chatted with them about all the interesting animals she saw there and all the stuff she had been learning about them in academy classes.

The hour was growing late, and they decided to head home, leaving Bain to his new apartment. Harper tearfully smiled at him giving him a tight hug.

"Mother, I'll be fine. I promise."

"I know," Harper said swiping at a stray tear. "I just know I'll miss having you home. But I understand why you're doing this," she quickly added.

"You can come see me anytime you want," Bain said, looking at her watery eyes.

"Don't think I won't," Harper smiled brightly, poking him in the chest.

Everyone said goodbye, with Bain promising to pick Wynne and Seadon up Friday after work. They would visit LARS and then the two of them would spend the night with

Bain. They both excitedly agreed, with the permission of their parents.

When Harper, Wilkins, and the children returned home, Harper grabbed a bottle of wine and a glass, and went outside on the patio overlooking the bay and just sat to think.

After seeing the kids off to bed, Wilkins soon joined her.

"Harper are you all right?" he said, sitting down beside her on the large swing.

"Yes. I guess I was just hoping to put this whole moving out thing off for a while."

"I know. But at least we have them back in our lives. We can't stop them from growing up."

"I know that. I just wanted to halt the process for a bit longer," she said, stiffly grinning up at him. "Anyway, we have another problem to deal with. Seadon hates academy here. He's bored stiff."

"What can we do about that?"

"I don't know. Maybe you can talk with your father about giving him more time with Captain Easton."

"I'll do that tomorrow and see what we can come up with."

"Maybe his going to LARS with Bain and Wynne will be a good thing. He thinks learning about wildlife is a waste of time."

"I can understand that. Boys, especially thirteen-year-olds, have a one-track mind. Whatever track their mind is on at the time is the only thing that matters." Wilkins laughed, remembering his own teenage years.

Harper laughed along with him.

"Well, hopefully the chat with Aaric will take care of Seadon. Now we have to worry about Wynne and little Adda. Wynne shows no signs of a talent yet and I know it bothers her. I can see the look on her face every time someone asks her about her plans for the future."

"I'm sure she'll find it soon enough, and Adda will come into her own soon as well. Besides, I've known several late bloomers in the talent area while growing up. On this side of Zanchier, they don't put too much stock in your talent anyway. They actually encourage the children to find an interest to pursue, not base their future on what their talent reveals."

"Yes. But our children grew up in Martanzia where talent was all there was. We've only been here four months. It will likely take her a bit longer to put the old mindset away and relax. At least she has Mother and the theater to help her. Mother says she's quite good at acting. Perhaps that is her talent?" Harper smiled at the thought.

"That doesn't surprise me. Your mother did raise her for five years. I'm sure some of Gracelynn's flare had to rub off on Wynne. As a matter of fact, all of our children are rather outspoken and strong willed, except for sweet little Adda of course."

They both laughed at the thought.

"True," Harper chuckled.

The two of them sat outside drinking wine and relishing in the sight before them. The darkness of the bay waters, the sound of the waves lapping against the low wall, the lights of the city of Praxtingen twinkling across the bay reflected in the water's surface, and the thought of their sleeping children in the house behind them; minus two of course.

Chapter 4

Wynne's Gift

Wynne Brinley was deep in thought about things as she got ready to leave for the Loradin Animal Rescue and Sanctuary with her brother Bain. She was all of eleven years old, and had a birthday coming up very soon, which she worried about. Most children looked forward to their birthdays, but Wynne was a little concerned because she had yet to discover her talent. If she didn't discover it soon, she was afraid she would be sent to work in the mines and harvest fields at age sixteen like the lower class and other non-talent citizens. Of course, she doubted her grandparents or parents would allow such a thing to happen to her, especially now since they lived in Loradin.

There were many benefits to living in Loradin. Even the lower-class citizens of Zanchier who resided in the outer cities around Loradin had better lives than the rest of the lower-class citizens of Zanchier. She really liked living here. Ever since her family had moved to Loradin and she attended the Loradin Primary Academy she had been making friends. That was something she never really had at the Port Proud Academy. Perhaps it was because she had been shy and self-conscious then. Both of her parents had been taken from them early on by the government and they had grown up with their grandparents. Their grandparents had been kind to them, but it wasn't the same as having their own parents. Then, they found out her grandfather had been a crook and had been put in jail. She would never forget that day, seeing him in handcuffs and the look on his face as he passed by her while boarding the airship.

Wynne vaguely remembered the night they took her mother from them. She had nightmares for years. Not anymore, however, not since about four months ago when both of her parents had returned.

Another benefit to living in Loradin was they didn't focus as much on a person's talent so much as their interests. This is where Wynne was relieved. She hadn't discovered her talent, but she did enjoy going to the Loradin Theater with her grandmother Gracelynn and visiting the Loradin Animal Sanctuary on the outer banks of the city with her big brother Bain.

Bain had told her once that he discovered the facility completely by accident while out exploring Loradin shortly after moving here. So, ever since then, Bain and Wynne made a visit to the sanctuary every week like clockwork. Every Friday evening after Bain left work, he picked her up and off they went. Of course, Wynne figured she was more of an excuse for Bain to visit the pretty girl named Raila. Wynne noticed how Bain beamed when he was near her, and how much nicer he was to her than usual when Raila was around. They had always gotten along but Wynne used to be more of an annoyance to Bain, as told to her by Bain himself. It didn't bother her though, whatever got her to the animal sanctuary was fine with her. She enjoyed the trips with Bain too. They had never really had the opportunity to spend time together before with just the two of them. Of course, Seadon was joining them today which was okay with her too.

Yes, moving to Loradin had been a big plus in almost every area of her life. And she discovered that she truly loved being around all the creatures and learning about them in ways the primary academy at Port Proud had never instructed them. They had only gone to the sanctuary four times now, and Wynne was growing more attached to the animals being cared for. She felt an odd sort of connection to them. She had never felt anything like it before. It was almost like she could sense what they felt or thought; like they were speaking to her.

"Wynne, are you ready yet?" Bain yelled up the stairwell.

"Coming," Wynne yelled back as she hurried to finish up.

"Hurry up. We don't want to be late."

Wynne grinned at his words. *He* didn't want to be late to see Raila. She ran down the stairs to meet Bain and Seadon waiting in the foyer.

"Ready!" she announced with a bound off the bottom step onto the foyer floor.

Zanchier Book 2: Uprising

Bain cocked a crooked smile at her and ushered her out the door.

Harper yelled, "Be safe you three!" She smiled at how close they seemed to be getting lately and how Bain took her along with him every Friday evening.

They all yelled back before the door closed, "Bye Mother."

Wynne stopped abruptly when she saw the new two-wheeled module sitting by the curb.

"We get to ride that, Bain?"

"Yes. It's one in the new Voyager line of Modules the LSS tech team has designed. They modeled it after Finn's. They've only made a few and wanted some of us from the tech team to try them out first. Don't worry, it's safe, and fun." He smiled at his sister and brother.

"Totally cool," Seadon smiled broadly.

"Awesome!" Wynne excitedly grinned.

Bain slung his leg over the seat while Seadon helped Wynne get situated on the back of the Voyager. Seadon climbed on behind her and Bain pushed a button, bringing the Voyager to life. Wynne and Seadon both smiled brightly at the feel of it and grasped the side of the seat beneath them.

"Hold on tight to me and move with me on turns!" Bain yelled back to them.

Wynne obeyed and quickly wrapped her arms around Bain's waist as Seadon grasped the small bar at his back.

They took off through the Loradin streets as Wynne beamed at the excitement of feeling the wind and sun on her skin while riding the voyager. Not to mention all the attention they attracted as people watched the strange looking Mod riding through the streets.

Fifteen minutes later, they arrived at LARS and Bain parked the Mod. They climbed off and Wynne ran to the doors, threw them open, and ran toward the back of the building smiling and greeting those she passed along the way. She flew out of the back doors, her attention on one particular creature this evening. Her sudden appearance grabbed the attention of Raila Orman and Dr. Patrice Barrister, the attending animal physician at LARS.

Wynne waved an excited hello to the two of them and stopped in front of a small, fenced area. She knelt down and reached over the fence to pet the extremely fuzzy, pink-nosed creature called the Trefell. LARS employees had found the creature lying beside the lake one day while out scouting. It had an injured paw and had been dehydrated. It had only been at the facility for a few weeks and was due to be released soon.

The ball of fuzz seemed to follow Wynne with every move she made.

Dr. Barrister watched with interest.

"Hello, Bain," she greeted the young man. "Who's this you brought with you," she asked motioning to Seadon.

"Dr. Barrister," he smiled back. "This is my brother Seadon."

Bain looked at Raila. "Hello Raila," he nodded and smiled brightly.

Raila smiled back. "Hello Bain."

Dr. Barrister smiled at the exchange between the two young people.

"Hello Seadon, nice to meet you."

"Thanks. You as well," Seadon replied, marveling at all the animals in fenced areas.

Dr. Barrister turned back to Bain, motioning to Wynne. "I do believe that your sister Wynne has a very unique ability. I've never seen creatures take to anyone like they do her. I think they understand what she's saying to them."

Bain looked at Dr. Barrister and then at Wynne. "Probably just appears that way. It's not like she can *really* talk to them," he laughed.

"I'm not so sure about that. I'd like to conduct some experiments if you and Wynne don't mind?"

"I don't see why not, as long as Wynne doesn't get hurt."

"Oh, no, nothing like that. I just want to see how the other larger creatures react to her. She'll be kept at a safe distance."

"All right," Bain replied. "Wynne," he called to her, "come talk to Dr. Barrister for a minute, will you?"

Wynne smiled at the fuzzy creature and gave it one last stroke before rising and going over to them.

"Hello Dr. Barrister," Wynne greeted the woman, smiling as she stopped in front of them.

"Wynne, I'd like you to follow me. We've acquired a new addition to the facility, and I would like to show you."

"All right," Wynne beamed, excited to see the new creature.

They came to a rather large, fenced area with a fenced roof, in which, stood a very young Kabihanxu. It didn't even have its adult feathers yet. Fuzzy colorful down stuck out in all directions from beneath its wings and under its tail. It was even still a bit clumsy on its four legs.

"Oh, my goodness! Wherever did you get that?" Wynne exclaimed.

Bain was shocked. "Is that a Firebird?"

Dr. Barrister grinned. "Yes, a very young one."

"Isn't it dangerous to have one so close to the city? They breathe fire don't they?"

"Yes, the adults do. So far, this little guy hasn't. We've aged him around four weeks old."

Bain was unable to take his eyes off the striking creature. Even at four weeks old, it was as big as a fully grown Yarequu. The firebird plucked at the downy feathers underneath its wing, pulling at the down with its beak and spreading its large wings, flapping to loosen the feathers. Colorful down flew everywhere in the cage. A large, teal, and golden feather floated to the ground in the cage just in front of Wynne. She reached through the fence to pick up the beautiful feather that was nearly as long as her arm.

Bain watched the look on Wynne's face. He had never seen her so in awe over anything before. He looked at Dr. Barrister.

"Where did you get it, and what exactly do you want Wynne to do here?" he asked a bit defensively.

"Don't worry Bain. She won't be harmed. The Kabihanxu juvenile is actually very friendly. We found him at the base of a large tree near the southern region of the Carpasian Mountains just west of Overton Colony on the edge of the Marshlands. I believe he was abandoned by his parents. Or he tried to fly too early. Needless to say, we watched carefully from a distance for several days and no other Kabihanxu ever returned for him. So, we stepped in and darted him with a tranquilizer to safely move him and brought him here."

"What do you plan to do with him?"

"Release him when he is old enough to care for himself."

"What if he comes back here?"

"We've thought of that. We plan to relocate him to Bakrashan and the Xantifal Mountains. It's a ten-hour journey from here by transport Module, four hours by boat, and probably just over a two-hour flight for a fully grown Kabihanxu. We're hoping he'll settle in there nicely and not want to return."

Wynne smiled at the birdlike creature as it cocked its head in different directions to get a good look at her. It clicked and squawked lowly as if it were talking to her.

Wynne audibly spoke to the bird. "Hello boy. How are you today?"

The firebird squawked again, flapping its wings, and taking a step closer toward Wynne.

Bain placed a hand on Wynne's shoulder, ready to pull her away if need be.

Wynne looked up at Bain. "It's all right Bain. He won't hurt me."

"You don't know that Wynne. If it wanted to it could probably break through the fencing or set you on fire!"

"I just sense that he won't."

"That's silly, Wynne."

Dr. Barrister watched the scene before her. "I don't think it's silly Bain. I believe your sister has a very rare gift, one that I've only seen in a select few children. It's one of the reasons I started LARS."

"Wynne," Dr. Barrister questioned, "how do you know the Kabihanxu is a male?"

"He told me," she grinned at them. Everyone, except Dr. Barrister, stared at her in disbelief.

Bain turned to Dr. Barrister. "What do you mean by *a rare gift?*" he asked confused, watching Wynne closely.

"When I was younger, I had a friend who couldn't find his talent. But I noticed that when we played together he often had a special bond or connection to animals. He often spoke out loud to them and they listened and obeyed him. He just seemed to be able to connect with the creatures mentally. No one else ever understood him or his gift. They simply marked him as untalented and sent him off to work the mines. I never saw him again after graduation. That experience made me more watchful of others, especially those marked as untalented. Of course, not all children marked as untalented have this gift. These gifted individuals are hard to find due to their being guarded in who they let know about their abilities. I only know of a few others who I believe are like your sister."

"What do you mean 'like my sister'?"

"I believe that Wynne can speak to creatures."

"That's nonsense. No one can do that!"

"Yes they can. I have several students that can do the same, although, I've never seen such a strong connection like this before."

Bain had surely never seen anyone like that. But he had to admit, Wynne and the firebird sure seemed to be hitting it off. He watched her reach through the cage to pet the massive juvenile that now stood near the fence, its beak pushing up against the fence as it made a strange noise with each stroke of Wynne's hand. Wynne giggled at the firebird's reaction as the others watched the two of them in amazement.

"Where are these others who can communicate with animals?" Bain asked, unsure if he believed Dr. Barrister.

"I have seven other students that stay here, in a special area of LARS, that do just that."

"Why aren't they out here with the animals then?"

"They have other special studies during different times of the day. Now it is after academy hours, and they are having free time. Many like to take the public Module into the city to enjoy their downtime."

"If these kids live here, then aren't they older, like me?"

"No. There is only one who is your age. He graduates soon and will take a position here at LARS. The others are considerably younger. Three are much younger than even Wynne."

"Their parents let them live here, being so young?"

"Yes, their parents were more than happy to know that their so called 'talentless' children were gifted in another area. Parents can visit during weekends, and the children can even go home on weekends as well."

Bain watched Wynne. "Do you want to keep Wynne here also?"

"Well, it would be ideal for her to have the training and spend as much time as possible around the animals. She would benefit greatly from it."

Bain chewed on his bottom lip. They only got their parents back four months ago, and he just moved out a few days ago. He doubted that his mother would allow Wynne to leave home just yet.

"What about academy?"

"We would take that over. She needs special training. She can't get that in the academy. They do teach animal science here in Loradin, just not at the level that Wynne needs."

"I don't think my mother would allow her to move here yet. I'll talk to her and Father and see if I can bring her here every morning when I go to work."

"That would be splendid. And tell your parents that I would like to speak with them about this at their earliest convenience."

"All right," Bain said. He had forgotten all about Raila standing there. He might possibly get to see Raila twice a day if Wynne attended academy here, but he was more concerned about Wynne and how her *gift* might affect her future. Did the Loradin government and the LSS know about this place? Should he tell his grandfather, Aaric? Surely they knew about these gifted children. If not, they certainly would now with Wynne being invited to live and train here.

"Wynne, Seadon," Bain called to them, "time to go home."

"Oh, Bain, do we have to go now?" Wynne giggled at the firebird again.

"Yes. Besides it's almost dinnertime and I have to figure out what to feed you two."

"All right," Wynne sighed. "Goodbye Raila, goodbye Dr. Barrister. I'll see you both next week."

"Goodbye, Wynne," they both called, waving to Seadon as well.

Dr. Barrister looked at Bain one last time. "Wynne should start training as soon as possible. I hope to hear from you or your parents about this on Monday."

Bain shook his head in reply to the woman's request. He waved goodbye to Raila and they all left LARS for the short ride to his apartment only blocks away. He would have to speak to his parents soon about Dr. Barrister's offer to Wynne, probably when he took her and Seadon home in the morning.

Chapter 5

Gracelynn's Haunted Dreams

Gracelynn Fenore tossed and turned in her bed. After four months of living in Loradin she still had trouble sleeping. The betrayal of her husband Derek and the horrific circumstances of her daughter Harper's imprisonment still weighed heavily on her mind. Especially since her husband had a hand in what had happened to Harper and Wilkins. Not only were those memories still fresh and troubling, but there was something else haunting her sleep.

Several times over the last week, she woke in a fit of sweat and fear. She saw war and unrest most nights when she closed her eyes. Perhaps it was all due to the betrayal by her husband Derek that was still so fresh? His years of lies and unsavory relationships with awful people, all of which led to the selling of their only daughter and her family. He was now locked up in a Loradin prison, charged with treason, kidnapping, and as an accomplice to murder. Gracelynn only wished they could catch the other two men truly responsible for all of it, Raif Martray and Vonder Mortruff.

She still cried often over what Derek had done to their family. It especially hurt when she saw the unrest and constant watchful nature of Harper, who once had a zest for life. Now it was like she was just trying to make it through each day.

Harper didn't seem like she could ever relax. She pretended for everyone's sake, but Gracelynn knew her daughter. She noticed how often she still looked over her shoulder and scanned the area and crowds of people when they were out in the city. Her heart ached for Harper and the apparent, constant, battle that took place inside her. She wasn't necessarily fearful, just very uneasy.

Gracelynn blamed herself for Harper's problems. For years she overlooked Derek's practices each time he assured her that everything was fine, and it was just business as usual. If she had pushed him the way she should have, then maybe Harper and Wilkins would have never been separated and forced into servitude. Maybe Harper wouldn't have the mental, emotional, and physical scars that she now carried with everything that she had been through. Gracelynn was very proud of the strong woman she had become. She never would have thought that Harper would have been capable of the things she had to do over the last five years to survive. She doubted seriously that she herself could have survived half of what Harper had survived. And Gracelynn doubted that she knew everything. She was sure Harper still hid some things from her. Probably from Wilkins as well, just to protect them. Those ugly little details that was her life in Vassalage for so long. Then there was the running, training, fighting, changing of her appearance, and living alone in a tree at the top of Xantifal Mountain amongst the Kabihanxu and Pagorinxes.

Gracelynn shuddered to think on it all. She shook herself from the images that played over in her mind, threw back the bedcovers, and went to shower. Today she would go visit Bain, Wynne, and Seadon in Bain's new apartment. She would pick up Adda from Neitha and Aaric, just a few doors down the hall, stop by a diner on the way, and bring them all a large breakfast. She seriously doubted that Bain had much in the way of food just yet. Then, she would go see Harper and Wilkins for a visit, taking Adda home before heading off to the theater this afternoon for rehearsals, and hopefully getting to take her darling little Wynne with her. Yes, Gracelynn had a new full life, one she enjoyed thoroughly. If only she could just chase away the dark memories more often than not.

Bain woke to the sound of a knock on his apartment door. He looked at the clock and noticed it was eight a.m. It had been hard to get Wynne and Seadon to sleep last night, causing him to oversleep this morning. At least it was a Saturday, and he didn't have to work. He rolled out of bed to answer the door.

"Grandmother, what are you doing here so early? Hello Adda." Bain ruffled his sister's hair as she beamed up at him.

Gracelynn breezed past Bain, Adda in tow, and entered the small kitchen. "Just bringing breakfast, dear."

"Great, thanks. I don't have many groceries yet."

"I figured as much. Or furniture," she answered, her gaze sweeping over the nearly empty space.

"Yeah, I just haven't had time to go shopping yet."

"I would be more than happy to help you with that."

"Thanks, Grandmother. I'll let you know."

"Well, how about tomorrow. Perhaps your mother and I can tag along with you and make a day of it?"

"We can ask her later when I take the kids home."

Wynne and Seadon began to stir from their slumber with all the chatter filtering into the spare bedroom. They got up, entered the living room, leaving the spare bedroom and the pallet of blankets they had made on the floor.

"Hello grandmother," they both stated.

"Good morning sleepyheads," Gracelynn smiled at them. "Breakfast?" she asked, holding up the bags of food.

They both scrambled into the kitchen, starving after the meager offerings of Bain's pantry the night before.

Gracelynn and Bain both laughed, "Looks like we need to go grocery shopping as well."

"I think you might be right," Bain chuckled as he swept Adda into his arms and deposited her on the high counter being there were no stools yet. The five of them had a nice breakfast over conversation, then cleaned up and left to take the kids home. Wynne rode with Gracelynn and Adda while Bain and Seadon took the Voyager.

Bain grinned at the woeful look on Wynne's face at not getting to ride the bi-mod again. Three on a Bi-Mod had been a tight fit. He would have to remember that next time and take an actual Module. That was one of the perks of working for the LSS. They had access to most of the company's Modules.

They sped through the city streets toward home, with Gracelynn and the girls following behind. The boys, of course, decided to see just how fast the Voyager would go out on the winding open coastal roads. Bain Reached home much quicker than his grandmother, much to the enjoyment of Seadon who laughed out loud almost the entire ride.

They all had a nice family visit, sitting in the yard in the coolness of the morning. While the kids played in the yard by the seawall, Harper and Gracelynn visited with one another while Wilkins made a second pot of coffee.

Harper looked at her mother's face, noticing the tired lines around her eyes.

"Mother, are you all right?"

Gracelynn stirred at the question. "Yes dear. Why do you ask?"

"You look tired."

"Well, I guess that means I'm getting old," Gracelynn teased her.

"That's not what I said. Are you sleeping all right? I know you aren't used to being alone, and you do have a lot on your mind these days."

Gracelynn smiled at her. "True. I've also been having nightmares, which is something new."

"Like what?" Harper asked, sitting up with interest.

"I keep having a recurring dream about war. I see all of us, you and Wilkins, the kids, Aaric and the LSS, all fighting something. I'm not sure what or who."

Harper thought about her statement. She knew there was unrest in the majority of Zanchier, and that the Scaithers were gaining in power and influence. Her mother was just learning most of that. Perhaps it was just taking its toll on her subconscious.

"I remember once when I was a little girl, you wouldn't let me go to my friend's house because you had a nightmare about it. The house where I was supposed to go had a fire and my friend got hurt. Do you remember that?"

"Vaguely. You weren't injured so it isn't something that cemented into my mind. I used to have a lot of those sorts of dreams. Some came true, some didn't."

"Mother, have you ever wondered if you have the talent for premonitions?"

"Oh goodness Harper. I doubt that. I mean, if that were the case don't you think I would have seen something about you when you went missing, or your father's underhanded dealings all those years? Or that all, or at least most of my dreams back then would have come true?"

"Maybe. I guess it depends on what you're supposed to know, or how things are supposed to happen."

"You're starting to sound like Wilkins," Gracelynn said, smiling as he approached with a tray of coffee and fixings.

Harper smiled up at Wilkins, taking the offered cup. "Yeah, his optimistic viewpoint does have a way of rubbing off on me most times. Anyhow, it's worth checking into. You could talk to Aaric about it and see if he's heard anything about any straining relations with Bakrashan or Martanzia. There have been some uprisings and civil unrest amongst the lower classes because of the treatment imposed on them by the Zanchieths, and now, more so by the Scaithers. People are tired of the abuse and the governmental system that keeps most of Zanchier's population in the poorhouse, working for scraps in the Rhe Mines. They earn so little it's almost slave labor."

"Yes, I suppose I could do that. I'll give him a call after I leave here," Gracelynn said, sipping some of the hot liquid from the cup that Wilkins had given her. She watched the two of them snuggled on the large outdoor couch. She and Derek had been that close once, long ago. Her heart ached for what used to be, but she was happy that her daughter had the love of a good honest man. And that the two of them were living the life they were meant to live. However, if her dreams had any premonition giving clues, all of their lives were one day going to be turned upside down. She just hoped that her dreams were just that; dreams.

After Gracelynn left, Bain talked his parents into going with him to the waterfall he had found. They agreed, as long as everyone stayed together. They packed a lunch and made a day of the expedition. Bain and Seadon took off on the Bi-Mod while the rest of the family drove the family Module. They bypassed the Praxtingen Market and drove straight for the falls, planning on spending the day swimming and exploring the cave.

Wilkins and the boys decided to take the road that Bain had told them dead-ended into the thick forest. They were all three curious as to what may lay beyond, and why the road just suddenly stopped just past the top of the falls.

Bain looked at Wilkins. "Father, my friend Silus talked like there was something unique about these falls."

"What do you mean?" Wilkins asked him as they walked back down to the pooling water below the falls.

"I'm not really sure. He just said that the cavern held some interesting secrets."

"Well, boys," Wilkins said, looking at his sons, "let's go explore and see if we can uncover a few of those secrets."

All three of them sped down the mountain, racing for the cool water. Harper and the girls laughed at their silly antics. Bain dove in first, followed by Wilkins, then Seadon. They swam over behind the falls, crawling up behind them.

"Wait, we need light," Bain said, diving back into the water and climbing out next to Harper. He grabbed the LSS, water approved flashlight he had found in his father's gear and had brought along for the day. He dove back into the water as Harper, Wynne, and Adda followed behind him, anxious to be included in their explorations.

They reached the falls, climbed up the rock behind, and entered the wet cavern.

"Watch for snakes," Wilkins warned them all.

Harper had been through a lot over the last six years, but snakes she did not like, especially since she had her children with her. She immediately scooped Adda up into her arms.

Bain's flashlight was very bright. The LSS used only the best, mostly designed by their own technical geniuses. The beam from the light lit most of the cavern in the direction in which it was pointed.

Bain, talking out-loud to himself said, "Now, where would secrets hide?"

Harper looked over to where Wynne was and noticed her holding a rather odd-looking creature. She yelled loudly at Wynne. "Wynne, put that down!"

"Mother, it's only a baby Trefell. It doesn't bite."

"How do you know that?"

"They taught us in academy. They chew wood and prefer certain types of trees, and they live near most rivers, large streams, or bodies of water."

"What on earth is it doing in here?"

Wilkins looked at Harper to answer. "There's probably a nest somewhere, especially if that is a juvenile."

"What's to say the parents won't come charging? Especially since one young lady suddenly can't control herself from picking up strange creatures." Harper looked at Wynne commandingly, but with a grin.

Wynne smiled and set the animal down, watching which direction it went, hoping to find the nest. Unfortunately, it disappeared out of the beam of light into a dark area of the cave.

"Bain," Wynne said, "shine your light over there please," she said pointing.

Bain pointed the beam in the direction Wynne indicated, but there was nothing there.

Wynne looked confused. "It just vanished. Like it walked through the wall or something."

Bain smiled. "Wynne, you're a genius."

"Thanks," she smiled happily. "But why am I a genius?" she questioned her brother, as he walked in the direction the juvenile Trefell had gone.

The closer Bain got to the wall, the more he could feel a small breeze coming from somewhere. As he approached the wall, he reached forward to touch it, only to realize that what he was seeing was a wall further back from him. It was an optical illusion. The wall closest to him stopped and a dark passage lay directly behind it.

"I think I found a secret," Bain said, turning and smiling at the others. They all followed behind him as he ventured into the passage, curiosity getting the better of him. He soon came upon the juvenile Trefell and decided to follow the now slightly startled creature. It hadn't minded Wynne handling it, but it apparently wanted nothing to do with Bain. As they walked, they could make out a line of Rhenium and Ruthenium running through the walls of the passageway. The raw mineral glinted with tiny sparkles every so often. Bain could see a few more passages that branched off from the one they were on but, decided instead to follow the creature scurrying along in front of them. A few minutes later, they were standing outside the cave at the top of the waterfall. Except for a few moments, they never really felt like they were walking upward.

The lush green forest covered in beautiful flowering bushes and trees greeted them. Not only were they at the top of the waterfall, but they were on the opposite side from where their Mods were parked.

Wilkins let out a heavy sigh. "Well, isn't this interesting."

"Very," Harper said. "If I had known this was here, I might have used it myself back when I was on the run."

Bain looked at her. "Apparently Silus does, or rather, knows someone who does. I'll have to ask him about it the next time I go into Praxtingen Market."

"Please take someone else with you, Bain," Harper begged.

"All right, Mother. I won't go to market alone."

"Or come here alone again," she stated in a questioning manner.

"Fine. But I can't always have someone along with me everywhere I want to go."

"I know. It's just for a little while. Until I know that Raif Martray is no longer out to get me or any of my children."

In the moment of silence, Wilkins put in, "All right, everyone. What say we go have a bite to eat? I'm starving after all this activity."

Everyone agreed, and instead of walking back through the passage and the cavern, they decided to walk down beside the falls through the forest. They would have to either swim back across or walk all the way around the larger body of water at the base. They decided to walk it, no one feeling like getting wet all over again. After filling up on the picnic they had packed, they loaded up and headed into the Praxtingen Market to look around, grab a sweet treat, and to chat with Silus.

Harper wanted to meet the man who sent her son off into the woods on his own to explore waterfalls and hidden passages. She wasn't too sure how she felt about that. She knew Bain was adventurous. She had been the same way as a girl so she couldn't fault him for that. If it weren't for the fact that she knew Raif Martray probably still hunted her, she wouldn't be worried.

As they walked the market and chatted with Silus, Harper constantly scanned the crowds. She didn't know for what, but she watched anyway. At one point, she thought a man at one of the eateries was watching them. She tried to see his face as he pulled his cap lower on his head and continued to look at whatever he was reading. They all soon left for home, and Harper threw one last glance at the man. Yep, he was definitely watching them. She couldn't tell if she had seen him before, but he was interested in someone in her family. Harper would discuss it with Wilkins when they got in the car, but as they piled in and the boys mounted the Bi-Mod, the man had disappeared.

Cass Briggs quickly climbed the steps up to his second-floor room. He was certain Harper Brinley knew he was watching them. He chided himself for getting made, he had never been this sloppy before. Or maybe she was just that cautious. Now, after getting a good look at her, he wondered if her looks were why Raif Martray wanted to get his hands on the woman so badly. He had to say, she was a very attractive woman. He would have to be much more careful now that she knew she was being watched. He might just do a bit more digging into what was the real reason Raif Martray had a bounty out on her. He knew she likely didn't need the money with her parents being who they were, so her stealing from Raif was likely a lie. Normally he didn't care or get involved with the lives of his marks. But if he were going to separate this family, take these children's mother away, he wanted the truth about why Raif Martray was hunting Harper Brinley.

SG Boudreaux

Chapter 6

Hard Decisions

When the Brinley's returned home, Adda and Wynne needed naps. Wynne took Adda upstairs to lie down with her while Wilkins and Harper went to the kitchen to find something quick and easy for dinner. Bain and Seadon followed them into the kitchen, each of them settling onto a bar stool.

Bain took deep steadying breaths, knowing he still needed to discuss Wynne with his parents.

"Mother, Father, I have something to discuss with you."

They both stopped what they were doing and looked at him, noting the serious tone of his voice.

"What is it, Son," Wilkins asked.

"Is everything all right?" Harper questioned.

"Yes, Mother, everything is fine. It's about Wynne. It seems that she has a gift."

Harper looked puzzled. "What do you mean?"

"Well, at LARS, she seems to be able to communicate with the animals there. Dr. Barrister says she is gifted."

Wilkins grinned, "Well I'm sure it appears that way. She does have a way with animals. But gifted? What does that even mean?"

"Wynne claims that she can understand their thoughts and feelings. And I really think she can. I've watched her with the animals."

Seadon chimed in, "Me too. The animals are really drawn to her. You should have seen her last night with that Kabihanxu."

Bain kicked Seadon in the shin under the bar.

"What!" Harper and Wilkins both asked sharply while Seadon nursed his now bruised shin and shot Bain a dirty look.

"It was caged," Bain defended.

"They breathe fire!" Harper said, her voice getting higher with each word.

"It's a juvenile. Dr. Barrister says it's too young for that yet."

"I thought she was just looking at birds, or fuzzy little Trefells, and Tribhons. I had no idea she was exposed to such a creature."

"Mother, Wynne is in no harm. If the animals were dangerous then the people who work there surely would know that and take precautions," Bain stated, trying to calm Harper.

Wilkins questioned Bain. "Why do you think your sister is gifted?"

"Dr. Barrister thinks she is, and after what I witnessed today, I think she might be too."

"Me too," Seadon stated. "It was really cool to watch her. Learning about animals might not be so bad after all."

Harper grinned at Seadon and his sudden change of heart.

Bain continued, "Dr. Barrister wants to speak to the two of you as soon as possible." Bain threw in the last part as cautiously as he could. "She wants Wynne to live at LARS and attend academy there."

"No. Absolutely not," Harper protested, shaking her head and pacing.

Wilkins asked, "Why would she need to live there?"

Harper added, "She loves academy where she is and is making friends. She is much too young to leave home."

Bain replied, "There are seven other kids living there that are like Wynne. They range from my age and down. Dr. Barrister even said that three of them are younger than Wynne."

"I don't care. I don't know this Dr. Barrister. I'm certainly not turning over my daughter to this person," Harper protested.

"Her name is Patrice Barrister. She's very nice. She wants to meet with you and Father as soon as possible. I told her that you wouldn't let Wynne leave yet, but that perhaps one of us could drop her off every morning and pick her up in the evenings."

Harper looked at Wilkins. "I think we need to go have a chat with this Dr. Barrister right now. I won't get any sleep unless I do."

"Fine. Let's go. Bain, stay here until we get back."

"Yes sir."

Harper and Wilkins drove to LARS, inquired at the desk as to where to find Dr. Barrister, and went in search of the woman.

"Doctor Barrister?" Wilkins asked as they exited the building at the back into the open air. Harper looked around at all the caged animals.

"Yes?"

"I'm Wilkins Brinley and this is my wife Harper."

"Ah, Wynne's parents," she said smiling, extending a hand to them.

Wilkins took it followed reluctantly by Harper, who grinned stiffly at the woman.

"I see Bain has spoken to you about what I wish for Wynne."

Harper stepped up, "Yes. And your wishes aren't important. Ours are."

"Mrs. Brinley, please, I meant no disrespect by saying that. I only meant that Wynne is a very special young lady."

"Yes, we know. Although I don't know that I agree with you about her having some sort of ability to speak to animals."

"I understand your skepticism. Most of the other parents felt the same way at first. But believe me when I tell you, your daughter's abilities are unique."

Wilkins put in, "Bain said you had other children here like her. How does that make her unique?"

"Yes, there are seven others who actually live here that possess the same abilities that Wynne does. But hers is very strong, the strongest I've ever seen. There wasn't even an introductory period between her and the juvenile Kabihanxu."

"About that," Harper stepped closer, anger now evident in her body language. "You could have gotten my daughter killed. What gives you the right to decide such things without our permission?"

Doctor Barrister only grinned respectfully, "I did ask Bain's permission first. Besides, the juveniles can't breathe fire yet. Wynne and the firebird bonded instantly. They have an amazing connection."

"It could have bitten her hand off," Harper rationalized.

"Mrs. Brinley, I assure you, if I had thought there was any danger, I would have never allowed the connection. We handle these creatures all day long, and they have yet to harm any of the workers here. And no one working here has the abilities that the gifted children do. Wynne wasn't frightened for a very good reason. She can understand the animal's thoughts and feelings. I truly believe that she can actually speak with them."

Harper and Wilkins exchanged looks. Harper said hesitantly, "We can bring her Monday morning to see what this is all about. After that, we can discuss this further. But in the future, when things pertain to our children, I would appreciate a com-call first. I'll leave mine and Wilkins numbers with the front desk when we leave."

"I understand, and I thank you. I don't think you understand just how extraordinary your daughter's gift is. The Creator has given her this ability for a reason. We must nurture her gift for her future purpose."

Harper simply nodded at the woman.

Wilkins answered with, "We'll see you about eight on Monday morning. Will that be a good time?"

"Absolutely. Whatever you need. I live here at the institute with the other children. I can give you a tour of the facility if you'd like."

Harper declined. "There's no need for that. Wynne won't be living here. We may allow her to come train, but not to live."

Dr. Barrister shook her head in understanding. "If you're anxious to view her abilities, you can bring her back this evening. I can even introduce you all to the other children as well."

Harper and Wilkins looked at one another. Harper said, "I don't know. We'll discuss this and give you a call about it later."

"The front desk can give you one of my cards when you leave."

Zanchier Book 2: Uprising

"Goodbye, Dr. Barrister," Harper said with a nod. Wilkins nodded as well and they left, stopping at the reception desk to exchange numbers, then headed for home.

Wilkins and Harper decided to wait until Monday morning to return to LARS with Wynne. They chose to do some experimentation themselves and took the children to the park where all the birds often flocked. They decided to just let the kids wander through the park while they watched Wynne. Sure enough, every animal in the park seemed to eventually gravitate to wherever Wynne was at the time. She chatted and played with the birds and other small creatures, as if they actually understood her. If they had not seen it for themselves they would not have believed it possible.

Harper asked Wilkins, "Why have we never noticed this before?"

"Harper, we've only had them back for a little over four months now. It's not like we've been able to watch and learn about them since they were babies."

"True," Harper grinned up at him. "What do you think this gift means? I mean, why would she need such an ability. To talk to and bond with a creature like a firebird?"

"I have no idea. But if the Creator were going to give me a gift, I'd say that was a very cool one to have. I could see how it could be very useful. I mean, to talk to and understand creatures? Wow! She might even be able to control their behaviors. That could be priceless if we go to war."

Harper turned sharply. "She's not quite twelve Wilkins and yet you're picturing her off fighting a battle with a Kabihanxu in tow!"

"You know it's coming, Harper, and our children, regardless of their age, will be greatly affected. The Scaithers, as you well know, are ruthless. They don't care about age, classification, or gender, and their organization is growing alarmingly quickly. This could greatly help her; keep her safe. We can't always be there to protect them, no matter how hard we try."

Harper sighed, "I know. I just want a normal life, Wilkins, if only for a few years."

"I know how you feel. I just want to watch them grow up too."

Wilkins called to Wynne, Seadon, and Adda. "How about we all go grab some dinner at our favorite restaurant?"

They all heartily agreed, and the five of them took off for Riker's Diner. After dinner, they stopped to grab a treat at a local bakery, then headed home.

The next morning being Monday, they saw Seadon off to academy, promising him a visit later that day with the academy director. Then Wilkins and Harper loaded Adda and Wynne into the car and took them to LARS.

They walked into the large, elongated building with the front and rear glass walls, through the lobby area, and out the back doors where they found Dr. Barrister and about ten others tending to the animals. Dr. Barrister noticed their arrival and went to speak with them.

"Good morning, Brinleys. I'm very glad to see you all today." She smiled at them in earnest.

"Good morning, Doctor," Harper said, grinning with trepidation.

Dr. Barrister motioned to the group tending to the creatures. "Let me introduce all of you to some of the LARS employees, and the other young people who stay here and train. They are all out working on some exercises with the animals." She led them over to some of the fenced areas and cages.

"Jerod, this is Wynne, Mr. And Mrs. Brinley and..." she motioned to Adda.

"Adda," Wynne quickly put in.

"Thank you, Wynne," she smiled at the enthusiastic young girl. "This is Jerod Narta. He is the oldest boy who trains here. He will be graduating soon and staying on here at the LARS facility."

They all said their hellos, shaking hands and making personal introductions.

"The other children are spread out about the facility working with different animals. I'll introduce you as we go. But what I would like to do first, is show the both of you how incredible Wynne's gift is. Would you mind following me to the Kabihanxu pen just over here?" she asked, pointing toward the right.

Harper looked at Wilkins apprehensively.

He gave her a reassuring grin. "Yes, Doctor, after you."

Zanchier Book 2: Uprising

They turned the corner around the building and a rather large juvenile bird came into view.

Wynne ran up to the cage and called to the creature. It enthusiastically hopped toward her, flapping its wings as down feathers flew everywhere.

Harper's heart leaped into her throat, worried the bird might harm Wynne. Wilkins put a steadying hand on her arm. Willing Harper to just watch and not let her imagination get the better of her.

Wynne stuck her arm through the cage as the firebird moved its head against her hand, making a sort of cooing sound.

Harper and Wilkins stood there in shock as little Adda pulled at the constraints of her mother's arms, wanting to play with the large birdlike creature as well.

"No, no, no, Adda, you can't get down here."

Wynne looked at Harper. "It's all right, Mother. I'll watch her. Besides, he won't harm her, I can tell. She'll be with me. He really likes me."

Harper and Wilkins walked over to the fence slowly, putting Adda on the ground but standing close by just in case.

Wynne looked down at Adda. "Look, Adda, just put your hand like this. He'll come to you," she instructed.

The girls giggled at the soft feathers of the large juvenile Kabihanxu, as they tickled little Adda's hands.

Wynne looked at Harper and Wilkins. "You can come up too and pet him. I told him that you were my family and wouldn't harm him."

They both moved forward carefully, still unsure of the large creature. Wilkins and Harper slowly stuck their hands through the fencing as one lone, large, eye contemplated the motion. The Kabihanxu turned its head toward them, and Harper instinctively pulled her hand back. Wilkins smiled and chuckled at the contact with the bird as he stroked the feathers on the crest of its head. Harper braved it again, sticking her hand through the fencing. She began to slowly pet the beautiful creature, the smile that spread across her face telling everyone she had finally relaxed.

After the interaction with the Kabihanxu, Wilkins and Harper had a slew of questions for Dr. Barrister about the facility, what Wynne would be learning if she went there, and where her classes would be?

Dr. Barrister gave them a tour of the entire facility, and by the time they were done, noon had come around. They stayed and had lunch at the facility with the other students and employees. Then, after much pleading from Wynne, agreed to let her transfer from primary academy to LARS effective immediately. Dr Barrister said that the LARS office would handle the transfer.

Wynne was beyond happy to be left at the facility while Wilkins and Harper went to FAZ to have a chat with the director about Seadon's future.

By the end of the day, Harper and Wilkins had seen to Seadon's transfer to the Airship Academy as well, a third level finishing academy. Harper was very apprehensive with it being outside of Loradin; just over the hills of Praxtingen in the Carpasian Mountains. The Loradin secondary academy, where he currently attended, agreed to send all his papers over by the end of the day.

Wilkins had already spoken to his father Aaric about Seadon's situation, and they had come up with a plan. Aaric assured Harper and Wilkins that an LSS agent, or two, would always be watching Seadon until they deemed it safe not to. They would screen everyone he came in contact with, students included. The LSS had already done a massive screening of the academy and all the students and teachers, which weren't many. Captain Matthews was the head instructor of the academy and knew to watch out for young Seadon. He was to be the youngest ever to attend the Airship Academy.

As Harper and Wilkins left FAZ that afternoon with young Adda asleep in the backseat, Harper's eyes began to tear up.

Wilkins placed a hand on hers.

She smiled at him, swiping at her eyes with her shirt sleeve.

"Sorry," she smiled. "Just realizing that another of my children will no longer be at home."

"I know, Sweetheart. But this will be good for him."

"I know...we can't hold them back just because I'm not ready for them to grow up. Even though they already have, and we missed it."

"We still have Wynne, and little Adda."

"Yes. But for how long? I'm sure that Wynne will soon want to live at LARS like the other students do."

Wilkins saw the pained looked on Harper's face. "We'll cross that bridge when it comes."

Harper shook her head in agreement and peered back at the sleeping body of her youngest as Wilkins drove them home. Wilkins would pick up Wynne by three and Seadon would be returning home by four through an academy transport Module. They would have a lot to discuss tonight before packing Seadon up for Airship Academy in the morning to move him in, giving him the day to acclimate to his surroundings. He was due to be at the academy by Wednesday morning to start classes. Harper leaned back against the seat and closed her eyes. She felt as though her life were falling apart all over again. Like she was losing her children once more, but she knew that wasn't so. She shot a small, silent, prayer to the Creator, just in case he was real and was listening. *Please, help me deal with this without breaking down in front of my children. I want them to feel free to pursue their own lives, with no guilt or reservations because of me.*

Chapter 7

Harper's Intuition

It was Tuesday morning, and Bain decided he would ride out to Praxtingen Airship Academy to see Seadon settled into the boarding academy. It seemed that Seadon had an entire entourage seeing him off. All grandparents were coming, along with Uncle Finn and Aunt Paisley, who was a recent addition to the family after a quick trip to the government building for a quick wedding two months back.

Bain figured that the large entourage had more to do with checking out the facility and getting an idea of the layout of the Academy in person for safety reasons. He knew a lot of what was going on being an employee of the LSS, and the fact that almost his entire family worked there.

He pulled the Bi-Mod to a stop, looking over his shoulder at the line of vehicles pulling into the academy's front parking area. He kind of felt sorry for Seadon having so many people here to see him off. It might make for an uncomfortable time of getting settled in. He figured bullies were bullies no matter their age, and that some might give him a very hard time about all of this. Especially since he was a few years younger than the normal, first year attendees.

Seadon, Harper, and Wilkins all stepped out of the family Mod and headed inside the office to check him in. Bain followed them while everyone else decided to roam the grounds of the academy, inside and out. Finn and Paisley took to walking the airship field and the outer hangers. Paisley also checked the outlying mountains around the facility, looking for points where any would be kidnapper could use to their advantage. She spotted a few areas and decided that they needed an LSS camera to be able to keep watch on the place.

"Pardon me, ma'am," came a male voice behind her, "but what exactly are you doing out here?"

Paisley turned to see a groundskeeper staring at her as she stared out over the surrounding woods.

"Just admiring the lovely scenery, and I am an avid birdwatcher. I thought I saw a very rare Teal-throated Rimtail."

"Oh, well next time just ask would you? Parents and strangers aren't allowed to wander around the academy. It's for the safety of the students, especially with rumors of wars and all."

"Oh yes, so sorry. I completely understand." Paisley walked off, having found where they needed to place the LSS cameras. She then went in search of Finn who was elsewhere doing the same.

Aaric, Neitha, and Gracelynn were helping to unload Seadon's things and taking them to his room. Aaric would install some small and hopefully unnoticeable cameras in Seadon's room and in the hallways of the buildings. His agents doing just that as they toured the academy with the director, filling the man in on Seadon's background and the need for more security.

Bain caught up with Seadon as they walked the hallways headed toward the dorm rooms.

"So, little brother, are you ready for all this?"

"Yeah, I think so. I can't wait to get inside the airships during classes. Even though we aren't allowed to fly them yet, it'll be great experience in knowing how it all really works instead of just what it shows in books and unworking models."

"I *meant* being away from everyone," Bain chuckled at Seadon's excitement.

"Well, I might miss everyone a little," Seadon grinned at his brother, "especially since we all haven't been together for very long. But I was bored crazy at secondary academy. I just couldn't take it anymore."

"Yeah, I get it. Just be careful will ya'? And don't take nothing from any bullies. There's likely to be somebody here that's going to give you a hard time just because of your age."

"I've never had any problems before. It'll be fine. Besides, I can handle myself," Seadon stated assuredly.

"Well, if you have any trouble, you can call me anytime. I'll always have your back."

The two of them smiled at each other as they entered the small, private room afforded him by the wealth of his family. His parents and grandparents insisted on a private room for him, just to be on the safe side. They were all wealthy but chose to live simply. And they all still worked for a living, mostly for the good and benefit of the people of Zanchier. Seadon was proud of who he was and where he came from. Well, except for grandfather Fenore of course.

Seadon looked around the room at the furnishings. There was a bed provided by the academy. The desk, lamps, shelves, bookcase, and icebox were all provided by his parents and grandparents. Being at the Airship Academy made him excited for his future. He couldn't wait to finish academy and join the LSS like the rest of his family.

He turned at the sound of his name and his mother's voice.

"Seadon, you know what I told you about the possible dangers from the people who took me and your father. Remember that, and stay on guard, all right?"

"I will, Mother, truly. I will be fine. I'll likely always be with other people anyway, and I'm sure that Grandad Aaric has placed enough cameras everywhere that there isn't likely a private place anywhere on the property." He smiled looking over his shoulder at the older man.

"Yes, and don't you forget that. You had better be on your best behavior or we'll know about it," Aaric teased him.

Seadon smiled brightly at his chiding. He was here just to study and learn. He wanted nothing more than to be an airman and fly airships. He didn't care if the LSS was watching; although the thought of never having any privacy *was* a bit daunting.

Wilkins stepped up to Seadon. "Well Son, it looks like we've got you squared away. It's about time we all get out of here and let you get familiar with the grounds."

Seadon smiled and hugged Wilkins. "Thanks, Father, for letting me do this."

"You're welcome," Wilkins said, leaning back and placing his hands on Seadon's biceps. He grinned down at his son and then stepped back to allow Harper to say goodbye.

Harper stepped up and hugged Seadon tightly. "You have your class schedule?"

"Yes ma'am," Seadon replied with playful exasperation.

Harper giggled at the frustration in his voice. She knew she was being over-protective, but she couldn't help it. "If you need anything we are just a com-call away."

"I know, Mother. Thanks." Seadon smiled at her, hugged her tightly, and kissed her on the cheek.

Everyone said their goodbyes and left Seadon to his room. They soon left the academy grounds with Paisley heading back to LSS with Aaric to make plans for camera placement around the perimeter of the academy grounds. Neitha and Gracelynn were going to pick up Adda from Nanny Trea to take her out for the day.

Harper and Wilkins were heading into Praxtingen market to speak with Silus, Bain's friend they had met on their last trip there and Finn decided to ride with them. Bain tagged along as well since it had been nearly two weeks since he had spoken to Silus and been able to peruse one of his favorite marketplaces.

Half-an-hour later they pulled into the market parking area and climbed out of the Mods. The market was bustling with people this morning. They all headed straight to Silus's booth.

"Morning, Silus!" Bain yelled across the street, waving to his friend.

Silus smiled broadly at the sight of his young friend. "Bain! It's about time you came 'round for a chat." Silus extended his hand as the young man took it happily. Silus nodded his hello's to the rest of them.

Castor Briggs sat in his rented, second-floor room, overlooking the market square, still waiting patiently for another appearance by Harper Brinley. When he heard the boisterous hello from Silus to someone in the crowd of people, he jumped to his feet, ran to the opened window, and traced the sounds, spying the man and one Bain Brinley. He grinned even broader when he noticed Harper and Wilkins Brinley pulling up the rear. He scrambled to get down to the street before the opportunity to track them this time got away from him. He was tired of waiting around for his payday to show up. This time he was ready with fake identification and clearance to enter Loradin through one of his Loradian contacts. He could follow them everywhere they went, affording him ample opportunities. He grabbed his cap and glasses and bolted out the door. He found a place close to Silus's booth to be able to watch his target closely, his eyes fixed on Harper Brinley as he carefully watched from beneath his cap bill and sunshades.

"Silus, nice to see you again," Wilkins stated, shaking the man's hand.

"Wilkins," Silus replied.

"Silus, this is Finn Mobley. He's a friend of ours and a work companion."

Silus nodded understanding as he shook Finn's hand, "Mr. Mobely."

"Finn," he insisted, grinning at the man.

"What can I do for you folks today?" Silus asked, knowing they weren't here for a simple friendly chat.

"We were curious about the falls you sent Bain to a few weeks back."

"Discovery Falls," Silus stated. "I see you found the secret."

Bain looked at him. "What's the big deal about the cave behind the falls? It's just a passage that leads to the top of the falls out on the other side."

"Well, I guess you didn't follow the other passageway then?" Silus said in a hushed voice, looking around to make certain no one was listening.

"What about it?" Wilkins asked curiously.

"Well, let's just say there's more to that passage than what appears. We used it years ago, long before you three were born," he said, pointing toward Wilkins, Harper, and Bain. "It was a communications center for the rebellion. Back when I was about Bain's age there was the start of a battle between some power hungry Zanchieths who tried to enforce subjugate rule over the people of Zanchier. A large group of freedom fighters squelched that real quick like."

"I've never heard of such a war before?" Harper stated. Wilkins shaking his head in agreement.

Finn said, "I think I remember that. At least a little of it from my childhood. I always thought it was just a legend, tall-tales that the old-timers just gossiped about."

"That's because the rebellion took care of business quickly."

Wilkins asked curiously, "So, you said that this cave held a secret communications room. Is the equipment still there?"

"It should be. There aren't many people alive anymore who remembers it exists. There weren't many younger fellas' who were involved like I was. Probably because my pap was the head of the rebellion. He was also the one who help set up the communications bunker in that cave. Just him and a few of his pals."

"That could be why the LSS has never gotten wind of it," Wilkins pondered.

"Probably so. Maybe it can benefit the people of Zanchier once more." Silus grinned at them.

As they chatted about the impending wars that were soon to sweep over Zanchier, Harper, as usual, stole a cautious glance around the marketplace. Her eyes suddenly stopped on a man in a cap and glasses, peering their way. When he saw Harper look his direction, he quickly averted his gaze. Harper's breath caught in her throat. It looked like the same man who had watched them the last time they were here speaking with Silus. Her spine tingled as shivers overtook her body. She continued to watch him. When he dared another glance at them, her heart stopped. She knew that man. She had committed his face to memory.

Harper reached out, grabbed Finn's gun from his back holster, and took off after the man.

Castor saw Harper coming at him. She had a gun in her hand and was moving quickly. He reached behind his back, realizing that he had left his room in such a hurry that he had left his gun on the table. He stood up and took off running.

Finn spun around, feeling his gun leave its holster.

"Harper!" he yelled after her as he, Wilkins, and Bain all took off after her.

Harper ignored them and kept her focus on the man who was now running, trying to hide from her. He turned down an unpopulated side street between buildings, and she followed, the gun still clutched in her hand. She never uttered a word as she ran after him.

Finn, Wilkins, and Bain, all watched her disappear around a corner and soon turned the same corner as well, not far behind her.

Cass was stuck. The alleyway ended into a rather tall, fenced, area, piled high with lots of packaging crates used to transfer goods to the market, along with a few garbage receptacles. He stopped and turned toward Harper with his hands in the air.

As she walked toward him, gun pointed at his head, she said, "I remember you. You're the man who pulled my screaming, crying, children from my arms five years ago. I swore I'd never forget your face."

Cass cringed as Harper quickly walked closer and put the gun only inches from his head.

Finn grabbed the gun, pulling it upward just as she pulled the trigger.

Cass screamed in fear, soon realizing he was still alive.

Finn looked at Harper, then at Castor Briggs. He didn't need to ask questions for they all heard what she had said to the man she nearly just killed.

Cass nervously stated, "No wonder Martray's got a bounty on you, lady! You're crazy!" he directed at Harper angrily, trying to compose himself after the near-death experience.

Harper pulled back her right fist and punched him in the nose as hard as she could. Sending his head backward and making him fall into some of the crates.

"Ow...!Son of a...!" he trailed off, scrambling back to his feet, and holding his now bleeding nose.

Finn grabbed Harper and spun her around as she still struggled to get at the man again. Finn handed her kicking, flailing, body off to Wilkins who tried to calm her down. Bain stood in shock. He had never seen his mother so angry.

"Cass, I suggest you keep your snide comments to yourself and tell me what you're doing here," Finn instructed his one-time friend from his life long before the resistance.

Cass looked at the older man whom he used to look-up to. "Fine. Just...keep her away from me, will ya'?"

"That all depends on what you say. Frankly, the only reason I stopped her was for her benefit," Finn stated plainly.

Cass looked at him then glanced around the alleyway at the others who watched him closely, waiting to hear what he had to say. Harper glowered at him, still breathing heavily with anger.

"Martray's got a contract out on her. Any of the Brinleys really. But he especially wants her brought in," he said, nodding toward Harper and still holding his bleeding nose.

"Still selling your soul to the highest bidder," Finn said, shaking his head.

"You're one to talk!" Cass said sarcastically.

"Things changed for me a long time ago, Cass, and you know it. You also know why."

"Yeah well, not all of us bought into that Creator stuff."

Finn looked at him sternly. "Get a move on, Cass. You're coming with us."

"Oh yeah? You mean I get a personal invite into Loradin? Where exactly are we going? You takin' me out to lunch?" Cass asked with sarcasm.

"You'll see." Finn practically dragged the man to the Module and put him in the back seat. "Now, if you try to get away I will not hesitate to put a bullet in you to slow you down. So just cooperate and we'll get along just fine."

Finn looked at Harper. "You ride with Bain on the Bi-Mod. I don't want you anywhere near Castor Briggs."

Harper still hadn't said a word, she just nodded at Finn and glared at the man in the back seat.

Bain looked at his mother as Finn and Wilkins took off in the Module headed toward the LSS building.

"Mom, are you all right? I don't think I've ever seen anyone that angry before. You nearly killed that guy."

"And I would have succeeded if Finn hadn't stopped me," she said, swinging her leg over the Bi-Mod behind Bain.

Bain turned to look at her. "I guess I just never thought of you as being capable of doing something like that."

"There are a lot of things I would have never been capable of doing had it not been for men like Raif Martray and Castor Briggs. I'm not proud of it Bain, but people are hunting us, and I promise you, Castor Briggs won't be the only one."

"I get that now. I guess I just didn't understand how serious things really were. I have to say though, seeing you punch that guy in the nose and sending him sprawling into those crates was pretty awesome. The guy is nearly twice your size. I didn't know you had that kind of power in such a tiny frame." Bain smiled appreciatively at her.

Harper chuckled slightly at him. "Let's go, son. I want to be behind the interrogation glass when Finn starts questioning him."

"Yes Ma'am." Bain smiled again, started the Bi-Mod, and they took off toward Loradin.

Chapter 8

The Bounty

Castor Briggs sat in the interrogation room at LSS headquarters, his laced fingers twiddling as he leaned back into the chair and propped his boots up on the edge of the table at which he sat.

Paisley entered the small room, instantly catching Cass's attention as he watched her walk in. She turned around in front of the one-way mirror and sat on the edge of the table, her long legs crossed at the knee.

"Mr. Briggs," Paisley began.

"Call me Cass," he interrupted, smiling brightly at the extremely attractive woman across from him, placing his feet on the floor to sit up.

"Mr. Briggs," she said flatly, "tell me about the bounty offered for Harper Brinley."

"If I had known my interrogator would be so attractive, I'd have asked to start sooner and get this over with."

"Mr. Briggs, just answer the question," she said, ignoring his words.

Cass leaned onto the table; his arms crossed casually in front of him. "What say you and I go for a little drink when this is all over?" he smiled, expecting her to agree.

Paisley stood up and leaned over the table, looking him in the eyes. "You know the little punch to the nose that Harper gave you that made your eyes go all watery? Well, *Mr. Briggs*," she emphasized his name, "if I choose to hit you, I promise it'll do a lot more then make you tear up and bleed a little. I dare say, you'll need a doctor, and quite possibly reconstructive surgery. Now, don't make me send you to the hospital to have your jaw wired to hold it into place."

Cass smiled at her threat but leaned back into the chair anyway.

Finn watched the scene from behind the two-way glass with amusement, then walked around the corner into the room leaving Wilkins, Aaric, and Harper in the observation room.

"Hello darling," Paisley smiled brightly.

"Darling?" Cass questioned, looking back and forth between the two of them.

Finn smiled at her.

"Cass, meet my wife," he stated, turning to Castor.

"Well now, Finn, it appears you found more than a new career."

"Just blessed I guess."

"I'd call it luck. You always were lucky."

"You know that to be a lie."

"Well, what happened to your family was just plain rotten. Evil what they did to your wife and kids. But that's why I never get involved." He turned to Paisley, "Of course, if there was another woman out there like you, I might make an exception."

"Enough, Cass," Finn warned, exasperated with his flirting. "Tell us about the bounty on Harper, and you mentioned it included *any* Brinley."

"I don't know what she did to Martray, but he wants her really bad. He's offered 100,000 rhedon for just her. Fifty thousand for anyone else. It's a real family affair."

"Why, what does he plan to do with her if he gets her?"

"He didn't specify, but I doubt it's to offer her a place in his organization."

"Cut the crap, Cass. You and I both know that you are more meticulous than that. When you hunt someone, you want details. You used to have more of a conscience and only hunted the criminal minded."

"Yeah well, the days when information mattered are gone. We're all just trying to survive out there, Finn. The 'whys' are no longer important. After they forced us to rip families apart eight years back, and the things I've had to do to get by, the whys aren't important. Harper Brinley wasn't the only mother whose children I had to take. Believe it or not, she's one of the few lucky ones. Most of the kids that were taken were executed. Of course, she is the only mother to try to kill me. Can't say that I blame her though."

Zanchier Book 2: Uprising

"Why did they spare her kids?"

"Orders from someone high up. They said that if she or the kids were injured or harmed, we'd all be executed."

"So, you actually executed women and children for Raif Martray?"

"Not me. I refused to shoot a kid. Took a few beatings for it too. The only reason they didn't kill me then was because I was such a good shot. My reputation as a government assassin preceded me in my next line of work. Plus, I never had any family for them to dangle in front of me as leverage. Besides, we all thought our orders came from the military. That's how it appeared. Raif Martray has his fist wrapped around the throats of some pretty prominent people. The man literally calls all the shots. If you and this little organization you now work for want to make things right in Zanchier, then you need to figure out a way to take out Raif Martray."

"Believe me, nothing would make me happier."

"Word on the street is Raif was the one who ordered your family killed. Is that true?"

"From what I'm told, yes."

"Sorry, Finn. I know you once thought him your friend."

"That was a long time ago. Before the resistance, and before I knew him to be what he actually is. I just wish I had known then that he had been the one responsible. I would have taken care of him long ago. Now, just finding the man is proving to be difficult. I don't suppose you know where he's hiding out?"

"Nope."

"Where were you supposed to deliver Harper or the others if you succeeded in locating and apprehending them?"

"There are some old, abandoned bunkers out in the northwest mountains of Bakrashan, on the lower, more desolate side. She was to be dropped inside one of the bunkers and the door locked."

"How would they know that you put her there?"

"There is a certain e-link all the bounty hunters use to signal success."

"How were you to get paid?"

"The money is supposed to be in the bunker when you drop the catch. I just make the switch."

"Meaning, someone is watching from somewhere. Or else any of the bounty hunters vying for the catch could just walk up and take the money. You said, Bunkers. How many and how do you know which one?"

"All I know is there are a lot of them. Maybe ten or so. After we send the e-link that we've apprehended the target, we are told which to use."

Finn and Paisley looked at one another. "Stay put," Finn said to Castor, "we'll be right back." He and Paisley walked out and into the observation room to discuss what to do.

Finn looked around the room. "This would be an excellent opportunity to get to Martray. If we plant someone in the bunker, then follow them when they pick her up, then we could catch him."

"I'll not allow Harper to be used as bait," Wilkins stated.

"Not Harper, another agent disguised as Harper. With Kamsten working for the LSS, she can make nearly any of the more highly trained agents to look like Harper. I'm pretty sure she said she had a few of the new Image Enhancer devices ready to use."

Aaric looked at Finn, "That might be a good plan, but how do you know this Castor fellow is telling the truth?"

"If not, I'll shoot him," Finn stated. "And he knows that."

"Well, this seems like our best opportunity so far," Aaric agreed. "I'll get one of our top agents on this. We'll discuss mission plans later this afternoon. First, we need to do a few tests to see if Kamston's I.E.s work. Treat Mr. Briggs to lunch and discuss the plan with him. He doesn't need to know all the details, just the basics. After lunch, bring him back here and we'll put him in one of the relaxation rooms until we work out the details."

"What do we do with him after that?" Wilkins asked. "We can't just let him go. He might not return when needed or possibly contact Martray and tip him off."

"I don't think so, Wil," Finn stated. "There's no loyalty for Martray from Briggs. But you're right about one thing, if we let him go, he might run. He can stay with me and Paisley. We'll watch him until we can implement the plan. Besides, it will likely only be a day or two."

"Let's hope," Paisley remarked, "I don't wish to deal with him anymore than necessary. He gives me the creeps."

Finn grinned at Paisley, "He talks a big game, but he's essentially harmless. I've never seen him actually harm a woman."

"Oh, I'm not worried darling, just annoyed by him," Paisley grinned.

Finn smiled appreciatively at Paisley's confidence.

Harper's reply wasn't one of amusement. "Well he was trying to take me, Wilkins, or any one of my kids, and that makes him very dangerous in my book."

"You are a job to him Harper. Even though he was trying to catch you, I don't believe he would have hurt you or anyone else," Finn assured her.

"Maybe not, but he would have handed us over to Martray, who would do significantly worse to any one of us. Especially me since I destroyed the weapon and ruined his plans."

"Yes, you have a point," Aaric answered. "Let's get on with the day. Wilkins, Harper, and I, will see to Harper's double. I have just the agent in mind. I'll also send a team out to scout the area of Bakrashan and these supposed bunkers Mr. Briggs mentioned. If we get things squared away today, then we may attempt the mission tomorrow."

Everyone parted ways with Finn and Paisley taking Castor to lunch at a nearby establishment, Castor looking over his shoulder the entire time.

Finn asked him, "Who are you looking for, Cass?"

"No one particular. Just that, if I'm seen with you, it could blow my whole career. Especially if certain people know you to be with the LSS."

"I assure you, there are no loyalties to Commander Raif Martray here," Paisley stated.

"Perhaps not, but before you all brought me into the city I already had clearance to enter," Cass stated.

"How?" Paisley asked, shocked.

"It's all in who you know," Cass stated, looking at her.

Finn asked, "I thought Loradin was impregnable to any outsiders?"

"As did I," Paisley said seriously, shocked that Cass was able to get clearance.

"No place is impregnable, Finn. You should know that. As assassins for the government, we could get into any place."

"We were never able to get into Loradin before," Finn stated.

"We never had a reason to try," Cass grinned slyly.

Paisley sighed. "Surely you're lying."

"Check me out. You'll see that I already had clearance to enter Loradin."

"I'll need to notify Uncle of this possible development. We'll need to take stronger precautions now I suppose. Who gave you your clearance?" Paisley demanded.

Cass shook his head. "Now, I can't be giving you my contacts. That would be breaking a very serious code amongst my kind. Besides, if I give away all my secrets, I'll be out of business. No one will work with me again, and frankly, my contacts are a major necessity."

Finn looked at him with seriousness. "Perhaps it's time you change your profession, Cass."

"We're not all as lucky as you, Finn," he stated in annoyance.

"I told you, it has nothing to do with luck. My path is already laid before me, I just have to be willing to walk it."

"Yeah, yeah, whatever, man. Look, I'm starving. My breakfast *was* interrupted this morning."

Finn knew that Cass was deliberately changing the subject, just as Harper always used to do, and Finn had noticed a change in Harper over the last few months. Maybe the Creator had dropped Cass in his lap for a reason. He wouldn't say that he and Cass had been good friends back in the day, but they had been regular acquaintances who had greatly respected each other.

They ordered their lunch and ate in relative silence, deciding not to discuss the plan to capture Raif Martray now that Loradin was suspected to not be as safe as they thought it to be. They soon returned to the LSS building, dropped Castor off into one of the relaxation rooms and locked the door. Finn and Paisley then headed toward Aaric's office for more details about the plan. When they entered Aaric's office, Wilkins, Harper, Mariska, the agent who was to pose as Harper, and ten other agents, were already there ready to discuss details.

Aaric started the meeting as soon as Finn and Paisley entered. "I've already dispatched a team to scout the mountains and bunkers. They were already stationed in Bakrashan doing some surveillance, so it shouldn't take them long to give us feedback about the area. Mariska will go to the lab after this and try out the new I.E.s Kamsten invented. We got a little taste this morning, but we want to see how long and stable the device is. She'll be wearing the thing all day around here, and we'll see how others, not included in mission details, react. Harper, I want you to either go home, or stay hidden. I want to see if we can fool everyone here. Mariska is a bit taller and built slightly different than you are. I'm curious to see how well we can fool everyone."

Harper stated, "All right, I need to go take care of a few things anyway. I'll leave after the meeting."

"Wilkins," Aaric put in, "you can go with Harper." Wilkins shook his head in acceptance, knowing she probably shouldn't be alone today after all that had transpired this morning.

"Tomorrow morning, if all the testing works well, we'll have Mr. Briggs send the e-link about apprehending Harper. Then he'll take Mariska to the bunkers and drop her as instructed. Our agents will wait in hiding until she is picked up. If Martray wants her as badly as it appears he does then we shouldn't have to wait long. We may even implement using MADS instead of the airship for traveling."

Finn was a bit nervous about that. "I've never used a Matter Arranger Device before. I'm not sure I like the idea of my body being split into millions of little pieces and put back together somewhere else."

Paisley smiled at his discomfort. "It's not as bad as all that. You won't feel a thing. It's like closing your eyes for a second and opening them to different scenery."

"Still, the idea makes me a little nervous."

"Yes, but it's a much faster way of travel. Many of the Zanchieths use the technology daily and have no issues."

"Yeah…yeah…, I know," Finn replied, still unresolved to the idea.

Paisley leaned over and whispered, "We can practice later if you like." She grinned and winked at him.

Finn only smirked in reply.

Aaric continued the meeting. "After the drop, and Mr. Briggs clears the area, we'll wait and watch. If Martray picks up our fake Harper then we swoop in and apprehend the man. If someone else makes the pick-up then we follow until we have Martray in our sights. Everyone understand?"

The room erupted in, "*Yes sirs.*"

"All right, you're all dismissed. See everyone back here at 6 a.m. sharp."

As the room cleared, with everyone going in separate directions, Finn and Paisley filled Aaric, Harper, and Wilkins in on the security issues that Cass had told them about.

Harper and Wilkins soon left the offices for the garage, climbed into their Mod, and left.

"Wilkins let's go by LARS. I want to put my eyes on Wynne. I know Adda is safe with Mother and Neitha, but at LARS, just about anyone can come and go there. I just want to make sure she is all right."

"No problem, we'll head straight there. And don't worry Harper, we'll keep our eyes open. I know I made light of your feelings about being watched, but after today, I promise to do better with that."

Harper grinned at him in reply, not saying anything as they drove straight to LARS.

Chapter 9

On Their Own

Wilkins and Harper pulled into the LARS parking lot and stepped out of the mod. As they entered the front lobby, they could see through to the back of the building where the children were interacting with the animals currently housed at the sanctuary. Harper locked in on Wynne instantly, watching her handle a Trefell. She was speaking to the creature as its tiny nose twitched and it reached for her with its front paws.

Harper and Wilkins looked at each other, both amazed by the gift their seemingly untalented daughter possessed. They walked outside, drawing the attention of Dr. Barrister. The friendly woman smiled and headed in their direction. Harper had to admit, she did like the woman. From what she had seen so far of Dr. Barrister, she seemed to be friendly and mostly, unassuming, a very laid-back woman who was also gentle with the children. Wynne had only been attending LARS for instruction for the last three days, but she was so happy every day when she returned home. It made Harper more relaxed about sending her to the institute.

"Hello Brinleys," Dr. Barrister said, approaching them.

"Dr. Barrister," Wilkins acknowledged.

"To what do we owe the pleasure of your visit?" she asked.

Harper stated, "I just need to see Wynne today."

"Well, as you can see," Dr. Barrister motioned toward Wynne, "she is fine. She is a very promising student. She has such an amazing connection to all the animals."

"Good," Harper grinned.

Wilkins looked at Doctor Barrister and spoke in hushed tones. "Doctor Barrister…"

"Please, call me Patrice," she interjected.

"Patrice, we have a very sensitive situation to discuss with you. You see, the reason we moved here to Loradin is because my wife and I are basically in hiding. Some very bad people are after my wife, and quite possibly our children. We need Wynne to be safe. We think we may need to stop her training for a while until things get settled."

"Oh, I'm very sorry to hear of your troubles. But, if you're concerned with her safety, she will be fine. We have surveillance systems in place all over the facility, and I will alert all staff to be on the lookout."

Harper spoke up, "Thank you for the encouragement, Patrice, but I think I would rather have her home with me."

"Harper," Wilkins turned to her, "Wynne is thriving in this environment. It would be cruel to remove her from it."

"I know that, but someone else may be watching her."

Wilkins put in, "More than likely, they would be watching you and me. Maybe it would be in Wynne's best interest to let her live here at LARS. We can visit anytime you wish."

"I don't know Wilkins. She may not even want to move away from home. I don't know if I can handle losing another child."

"Harper, you're not losing your children, you're giving them space to grow. To become who they were meant to be."

"But we've only just gotten them back." Harper began to fidget, and her eyes began to tear up.

Dr. Barrister interrupted them. "Why don't we go into my office to discuss this further in private."

Wilkins nodded. "Thank you, Patrice."

They followed Patrice inside the building and up a flight of stairs. From outside, the building appeared to be one story with high ceilings. The back half of the building, to the left of the wide reception hall, was a second story.

"This is where my offices, academy rooms, and the dormitory is located," she explained as they went.

At the top of the stairway, she turned left, and they walked back toward the tall foyer. They walked into an office that was connected to the solid glass back of the building. From Dr. Barrister's office they could see the entire backside of the LARS holding facility.

Harper watched in awe as the rescued animals and creatures roamed their cages, interacting with the children. They all laughed and played with the animals, talking to them like they would any other person. Harper grinned

Zanchier Book 2: Uprising

slightly as she watched her little Wynne interact with the massive young Kabihanxu as it followed her around the cage. They played together like a pair of siblings who had grown up closely together for years, with a familiarity that Harper herself didn't even feel with her children.

Dr. Barrister motioned to the chairs in her office as Wilkins and Harper sat down. "Now, I don't wish to pry, but there is obviously something of importance happening here. I only ask so that I can do my best to keep Wynne safe.

Wilkins looked at Harper who nodded her permission. He began with, "Well, it truly is a long story, but the short version is this. My wife and myself were taken from our children many years ago and only four months ago were reunited with them and each other. We were forced to serve the Zanchier government, or so we thought. She thwarted a plan by some very bad people who wanted to control and destroy anyone and anything that didn't agree with their ideals. Now, some very powerful men have a contract out on not only her, but our family as well, Harper being the most sought after. We are concerned for all our children. Even though Loradin is safe, we found out today that it isn't impossible for those in power to gain access to the island."

"Goodness!" Dr. Barrister exhaled. "Well, if that is the case, then whatever you wish to do I'll support your decision. But perhaps, if someone is watching you, Wynne might be safer here?"

Harper looked up at her words, "I'm not so sure. I can protect my children better than anyone because I am their mother."

"Yes, I understand that. But do you plan to lock her away in the house for an indeterminable amount of time? What kind of life would that be for her, or you? You know, with the rumors of war soon to break out, perhaps it's time I tighten the reins here at the institute a bit anyhow. We can begin some new protocols requiring the children to be indoors by a certain time, and not allowing them so much freedom in the evenings. I, or an employee, can accompany them at all times when they leave the premises. It is likely to become a way of life soon enough anyway."

"I hate to make you impose such rules and regulations on everyone just because of my family's problems."

"It's not a problem, Harper. The children need to learn that there is bad in the world. We've had it too good here in Loradin for many years. It doesn't surprise me that powerful evil men have wormed their way through the Loradin gates. I promise to do my best to keep her safe."

Harper chewed on her bottom lip as she looked at Wilkins in contemplation. Wilkins nodded his agreement with Dr. Barrister's suggestion.

Harper shrugged her shoulders and sighed. "I suppose we can give it a try. If at any time you think someone is lurking around or seems suspicious, please don't hesitate to call either of us. I will also leave a few other numbers for people who you can contact should we be unreachable."

Dr. Barrister stood and handed them a piece of paper and a pen. "That will be fine. And please, try not to worry about her. You can rest assured that I'll keep a close eye on her, and all who come and go through the facility."

Wilkins said standing, "Don't be surprised if you see a few people standing watch. We both work for a securities agency. If we have guards appointed here, we'll make certain they introduce themselves so as to not be suspect. We'll also call you to let you know who and when."

"I'll give you my personal com-call so you can contact me directly," Patrice answered.

Harper sighed. "Well, I suppose we should go discuss this with Wynne. She needs to know why we are making this decision. And if she agrees and wants to stay here, than she will need to pay attention herself to her surroundings at all times."

After writing down the contact information for Aaric and Finn, and receiving Patrice's personal information, they all left the office and headed back outside to the rehabilitation and training area to speak with Wynne. After explaining to her what was going on, she was very excited to have the chance to live at LARS with the rest of her newly made friends. Kids that were like herself, people she had something in common with.

Harper looked at Wynne, "We can go ahead and pick up your things from home and return you here tonight." Harper was saying these things, but her heart ached at the thought of Wynne living elsewhere.

Zanchier Book 2: Uprising

Wynne, ever the sensitive type, looked at her mother. "I can stay one more night at home, Mother. And, if it's safe, I can come home on the weekends."

Harper reached out and hugged her daughter, pulling her into her arms. "I don't know how I'm going to survive having my three oldest gone from me already?"

"We aren't gone, Mother. Just away for a bit. We are all still very close by miles. Besides, we'll always be family, no matter what happens."

"How did you get to be so grown up for one so young?" Harper giggled through her tears.

Wynne just smiled up at her Mother. She then turned to Patrice. "See you tomorrow Dr. Barrister." Wynne waved to her friends and then called out a goodbye to the Kabihanxu. The creature screeched in return, bobbing its head up and down as if waving, then stretched its wings for a good flap.

Dr. Barrister replied with a wave, "We'll have your bed ready for you in the morning."

They drove back to their home, contacted Bain to inform him of their decision and why, since he most likely would see Wynne more frequently than they would now with his trips to LARS to visit with Raila.

Neitha and Gracelynn were due to return Adda shortly, so while they waited for that, Harper, Wilkins, and Wynne, spent the rest of the afternoon together as they packed Wynne for her move to LARS.

After they were finished packing, Harper called and invited Bain over for dinner, then called for delivery from their favorite restaurant. Adda was soon returned home while Harper quickly explained the new changes to both of Wynne's grandmothers. They both wished her well and left them to spend the rest of their evening together.

Dinner was delivered fifteen minutes later and the five of them sat down outside along the water's edge to share a meal.

Harper sighed heavily as she watched her beautiful children and wonderful husband laughing and enjoying each other's company. If only Seadon were there to share in the joy with them the evening would be perfect. Harper knew that all of them being together now, in one place and at the same time would be much harder as they were all spread out, already living their own lives. The feeling of wistfulness and sadness threatened to take over and she shoved it aside. She wanted to enjoy this evening. There would be plenty of time later for her to cry over the loss of having a part in her children's daily lives. Thank goodness she still had her sweet Adda. It would be many years before she would leave the nest. Strange how the one child she never knew existed was the only one she had left to care for now. She looked down into the smiling, giggling face of the little girl in her father's lap. Harper smiled, shook off the dark feelings threatening to overtake her mood, and determined herself to join in the camaraderie around the table. She would not spoil Wynne's last night home with her pouting, pitiful, poor me attitude. Wilkins was right. Their brilliant, wonderful children had bright, successful futures ahead of them, and she would resolve to let them get on with their lives, wherever it took them. And if Raif Martray tried to harm her children in any way, she would hunt him down and take care of it herself if need be. She would do whatever it took to keep them all safe.

Chapter 10

LSS Resistance

The next morning, after dropping Wynne at LARS institute and making her promise to com-call that evening, Harper and Wilkins made it to the LSS building and Aaric's office just in time for the meeting to begin.

Harper was a bit taken back by the agent, Mariska, who now looked almost just like herself. She was a bit taller and more muscular, but if you didn't know any better, she could certainly pass for Harper, especially from a distance. Which was exactly what the LSS team was hoping for.

After they found a seat, Aaric decided to start the meeting.

"Now that everyone is here and accounted for, I'll get down to the details of the mission. Yesterday we tried out Mariska's new temporary identity. She wore the Image Enhancing Device around the office yesterday, and nearly everyone thought she was you, Harper." He nodded in her direction. "If we can fool those who know both Mariska and Harper, then Raif Martray and his associates shouldn't be too difficult to mislead. This morning we had Mr. Briggs send an e-link that he had apprehended Harper Brinley and would be in route today to drop her in the bunker. Our agents stationed in the area of the Bakrashan Mountains checked out those hidden bunkers in the northwest region nearing the desert. They all reported nothing unusual about the bunkers, only that they are well hidden, either underground, or within a freestanding rock bed. Which of these bunkers we are to place our fake Harper inside of remains to be seen. Those instructions are to be given via e-link once more. We are awaiting a reply any moment now."

Finn asked, "When do we head out. It's a long ride out that way. This is going to take all day."

"As soon as this meeting is completed, then everyone will be dispatched. Finn, you, Paisley, Mariska, and Mr. Briggs, will stay together until you reach the bunker site. At which time, Briggs will lead Mariska to the bunker, placing her inside." Aaric looked directly at Castor and said, "Make no mistake, Mr. Briggs, you will be watched thoroughly the entire time, and should you decide to do differently it won't end well for you."

Castor returned Aaric's steely look. "I have no intention of doing anything *differently*."

"Right. Then we'll all get along quite nicely," Aaric replied, keeping eye contact with the man.

Aaric turned to the group. "Agents will be placed in several different areas along the mountainside. Some watching the bunker where the drop will be made, and others watching the remaining bunkers for any surprises. You're all due to travel with the MADS after picking up your equipment from the tech department where your supplies have been readied. Good luck, and God speed to you all."

Harper asked, "Aaric, what about Wilkins and me?"

"Wilkins is appointed to the mission, but you'll need to stay here Harper. If anyone sees you out there, it could blow the whole mission and endanger Mariska's life even more."

She exhaled heavily. "All right. I understand." She then looked at Mariska. "Be careful. Raif Martray is an intelligent man. He won't be easy to catch. He's also an evil man who relishes every aspect of inflicting pain just for fun. He'll not hesitate to kill you."

Mariska nodded to Harper.

Aaric stated, "Hopefully Martray will be in custody before anything like that can happen. All right everyone, see you all downstairs in fifteen minutes."

Harper wasn't so certain about that. She could only hope that the mission went well. She wanted all of it to end. She was so tired of being hunted by this man, and now he was after her children. As everyone got up to leave, she looked at Wilkins.

"Please be careful, Wil."

"Don't worry. I've trained long and hard with the S.O. for missions like this, long before coming to work for the LSS. I'll be fine, I promise."

Zanchier Book 2: Uprising

Harper walked with them to the tech department where everyone donned there packs and MADS. Soon they would all be off, somewhere across Zanchier in search of a madman. She stood there for a while after they had all gone, now alone in the room as Maubrey, Cranston, and Winnie returned to their workstations. She turned and went back toward the on-sight gym to work out some of her pent-up anxiety. After that, she would enter one of the relaxation rooms and await news of how the mission was going, and maybe even do a little talking with the Creator on behalf of everyone who was risking their lives for her and her family.

While walking the halls headed for the gym, she came upon Bain who knew something was bothering her by the look on her face.

"Mother, is everything all right?"

"No. Your father, Finn, Paisley, and a woman who looks nearly identical to me, plus a whole slew of other agents just left to try and capture Raif Martray. I'm just a little stressed and worried for everyone involved."

"Well, do you want to get out of here? We can take a ride on one of the Bi-Mods," he offered.

"Sure, if I'm not taking you away from anything here."

"Not really. With the talent in this place, I feel sort of out of my depth here. Cranston, Winnie, and Maubrey are a cut above anything I've ever seen," he smiled.

"All right then. It would be a pleasure to spend some time with just the two of us. We haven't really been able to do that yet have we?" She smiled, slipping her arm into his as the two of them left the room, jumped onto a Bi-Mod, and set out to explore the city of Loradin and just enjoy the bright, partially cloudy, sun-streaked sky.

Bain steered the Bi-Mod skillfully through the streets, as people began to mill about and open shops in the early morning. Harper breathed in the scent of the water in the air, relished in the feel of the mixture of cool air and sun on her skin, and the fact that her eldest son sat just in front of her. All was right in her world at this one moment in time. If only it could be this way all the time. She felt more relaxed right now than she had in a long while.

Bain pulled the Bi-Mod to a stop in front of a local coffee shop and the two of them climbed off. They walked inside, ordered some coffee and breakfast, and walked back outside with coffee cups in hand to the umbrellaed patio tables which adorned the wide seating area just across from the lake.

Harper and Bain sat and watched the water sparkling in the sunlight. She inhaled deeply and exhaled, releasing some of the tension of the past few days.

"Thank you, Bain, I really needed a morning like this, with you." She smiled thankfully at him.

"Sure, anytime." He smiled brightly back.

The waiter delivered their meal, and they ate while they chatted about everyday life. Harper really needed the distraction, and the visit with her eldest child. After breakfast, they drove over to one of the beach areas of the island and thoroughly enjoyed a walk in the sand along the water's edge. By the time noon rolled around they were starving from all the activity. They went and picked up Wynne to have lunch and spend an hour just visiting with her. By the time Harper and Bain returned to LSS headquarters it was nearing 1:30 in the afternoon. She stopped by Aaric's secretary's desk, Kinley Peters, and inquired if there was any word on the happenings of the mission.

"Not much, Harper. The last I heard, they had arrived and made the drop but that's all I know at the moment."

"Thank you, Kinley. I'll be in the relaxation room just down the hall when you know more."

"All right. I'll com-call you as soon as I hear anything else."

Harper nodded and left the office.

Bain decided he would check in with the tech department to make sure he wasn't needed for anything. Then he would join his mother in the top floor relaxation room to wait with her. He was a bit anxious himself with his father being on the mission as well and decided that his mother could use further distraction. After all, she had been right about Raif Martray trying to find them. They all had figured she was just being overly protective, now seeing they all needed to pay more attention to their surroundings and those who took up space in their immediate vicinity. If it hadn't been for his mother's ever watchful eye anyone of them could now be held prisoner by Martray. He decided that he personally would do better, and he would go see Seadon this evening and warn him as well. Especially since he was living outside the Loradin city gates and the protection those gates offered.

Finn stood watching from his place in the trees as the scene played out before him, heavily camouflaged as part of the forest around him. Castor Briggs walked the now disguised Mariska down the mountainside toward the bunker. Agents were stationed all around every bunker that had been located along the mountainside, but several more watched the one in question. He looked over to where he knew Wilkins to be lying in wait.

Wilkins nodded ever so slightly at Finn. The I.E.'s developed by Kamsten Whitsler allowed the wearer to scan whoever, or whatever environment, they wished to camouflage too. Wilkins was shocked when they had arrived in the mountains and scanned the forest around them. When everyone disappeared into the surrounding foliage with a simple push of a button, they all sort of freaked out a bit, a few of the agents quickly pushing the button again to uncloak just to get their bearings for a minute.

They all watched as Castor placed Mariska into the bunker, picked up the bag of cash, and closed the door. He then scrambled out of the area as quickly as he could, knowing he wouldn't get far before being picked up by an agent. He made his way quickly through the trees trying to decide whether he wanted to take off and hide in one of the bunkers they didn't know about or allow them to return him to Loradin. Once Raif Martray realized that Mariska wasn't Harper, he would likely put a bounty out on him. He doubted the LSS would capture Martray today. Even with all their organization and skills, Martray was a clever man who normally stayed one step ahead of everyone else. Castor decided he would take his chances and disappear. He could live quite nicely on a hundred thousand rhedons. Finding the place that Raif Martray or Victor Mortruff couldn't reach was the real problem.

Castor opened the ground level bunker door and disappeared inside. The agent assigned to watching Castor walked over to the bunker, lifted the camouflaged lid, and peered inside. Castor was gone. The agent threw open the door, climbed down into the six-by-six hole, looking around for any signs of where he had gone. He noticed a small disturbance in the soil on one side. He looked around for anything that might be used as a lever, noticing a small root sticking out of the side of the wall. He pulled it, and a small door swung open slightly. He carefully pushed it open to reveal a dark tunnel, but no Castor Briggs.

He quickly climbed out and stated over their ear-coms. "Briggs has disappeared through an underground tunnel. Check on Mariska!"

Wilkins and Finn quickly left their hideouts and made their way cautiously toward the bunker in which Mariska had been placed. Wilkins swung open the door to find it empty.

"She's gone," he notified all the other agents through the communication system.

Wilkins quickly scanned the interior of the bunker, finding a similar lever which opened a door to a tunnel. He and Finn entered the tunnel, trying to track down where Mariska had been taken. Twenty feet inside the tunnel, they realized it branched off in four separate directions.

Wilkins spoke into his ear-com, "We need some help down here. There are four tunnels, we'll need help following them. Two agents per tunnel while a few more stay topside as lookouts. Quickly people, before anything happens to Mariska."

They were joined by several more agents and they all branched off to follow the dark tunnels. Wilkins and Finn took a tunnel which ran south according to the navigation system in their equipment. They followed it for what seemed liked miles, finally coming upon a door. They carefully opened it; their weapons ready for anything that might be on the other side. The door opened onto another area of the forest on the southern edge and opposite side of the mountain where they started.

Zanchier Book 2: Uprising

Wilkins surveyed the area, looking for anything out of the ordinary. "We must have walked right through the bottom of the mountain."

Finn looked at the outside of the door they had just walked through. It looked exactly like the rock-facing of the mountain that extended straight upward, blending in nicely.

"How old do you think these tunnels are?" Finn asked.

"Not sure. Maybe they are like the ones Silus told us about yesterday while we were at the Praxtingen Market?"

Finn nodded. "Could be. But if that's the case, it looks like Martray knows about them as well. There's no telling which direction they took her. If they came this way, I certainly don't see any other tracks to attest to that."

"Neither do I," Wilkins answered. "Let's just hope some of the other agents found Mariska, or which direction they took her."

"Let's find out," Finn stated, putting in a call to the others who were searching the other tunnels.

"Any luck," he asked.

"Not in the eastern tunnel," came a reply.

"No luck in the northern tunnel. It just dead ends. There has to be another way out," came the reply.

"West team?" Finn asked, but only received static as a reply. He looked at Wilkins, speaking into the com devices. "Wilkins and I are doubling back and heading west."

Finn and Wilkins returned through the dark tunnel as quickly as they could go. Once they arrived at the splitting point, they took the western tunnel, being as careful as possible, unsure what they were going to come upon.

Wilkins looked at Finn. "I have a really bad feeling about this."

"Let's hope that's *all* it is, a feeling," Finn replied, as they quickly but cautiously continued forward. It seemed like they had walked forever before spotting something lying in the tunnel up ahead. It was one of the agents. He had been shot and killed.

Finn and Wilkins looked at one another and carefully continued on. The other agent was nowhere to be found. They kept going forward, suddenly entering a space that seemed larger than the narrow tunnels, yet still just as dark.

They went in different directions to roam the small room, the clip-on lights on their weapons providing some light.

"Finn," Wilkins said, waving him over to a side wall. Finn joined Wilkins, looking down at the body of the other LSS agent, also shot. Wilkins leaned down to check his pulse.

"He's still alive," he said, making a call to the others. "We need a medic and stretchers to the western tunnel. Horton is dead. Braidon is alive but seriously wounded. Mariska is still missing."

Finn looked at Wilkins. "You stay here with Braidon. I'm going to continue on."

"Be careful, Finn."

Finn nodded his reply to Wilkins and searched the dark, cave-like room for an exit. He knew there had to be one similar to the one they had found at the end of the other tunnel. As he continued walking, he noticed a recessed wall and walked through the narrow crevice into another short tunnel, finding a door at the other end. Finn readied his weapon, pushed on the door easily, allowing only a crack to open as dim natural light broke through the darkness. When nothing happened, he kicked it opened all the way, weapon up, before walking through it. There was a large room built into the underside of a massive cavern. A small inlet of water sat in the center of the room and led out through a cavernous opening about a quarter-of-a-mile away to the outside of the cave. Small docks sat at the edge of the water, connecting to the ground. Old crates and some machinery sat against the walls. Some of it covered with large tarps. Finn yelled back to Wilkins.

"Wilkins, you gotta' come see this!"

It was only a matter of seconds before Wilkins appeared through the doorway, whistling as he entered. "This is some set-up."

"No kidding. I just wonder if it is Martray's doing, or if it is left behind from the last war Silus mentioned."

"We can find that out after we return to LSS headquarters. I'd say that Horton and Braidon came upon whoever picked up our look alike, and then they escaped to here, where a boat must have been waiting."

"I'd say that's a good assumption. I can smell traces of boat fuel in the air. The cavern holds smells a bit longer with the lack of ventilation down here." Finn looked up at bits of light filtering into the cavern from apparent breaks in the rock far above their heads.

"Let's hope that Mariska can take care of herself. I'd say this is one mission where we failed horribly. But, we had no way of knowing all of this was down here," Wilkins said, looking around.

"We didn't, but Briggs obviously did, seeing as how he used them to escape. And if I get my hands on that snake's neck, he'll regret leaving out these important details."

The two men left the area, making a plan to come back to explore further. Right now, the important thing was to get Braidon to the hospital and hope that Mariska would check in later to let them know she was all right. Harper would be very unhappy about this, as they all were.

SG Boudreaux

Chapter 11

Breached Borders

Wilkins called Aaric, who waited at the forest's edge along with a few other agents, to inform him of the events that had taken place. Aaric com-called the border patrol to search the waters and ask the neighboring coastal towns about any suspicious watercraft coming from that direction and time of day.

The slain agent, Horton, and the injured man Braidon were both brought back on travel gurneys and transported back to Loradin by way of the MADS. Aaric called an all-agent manhunt to try to locate Mariska before they were too late. They thoroughly scoured the area, especially the underground tunnels and where they led out. If they had brought the airship they could have flown over the coast trying to spot any watercraft on Everly Lake, but Aaric figured that whoever had taken off with the fake Harper was nowhere to be found.

Aaric was pacing the ground, thoughts flying through his head when Paisley com-called.

"We've searched everywhere we know too, but there is no sign of her sir."

"What about Castor Briggs?"

"He ditched through the underground tunnels as soon as he made the drop and picked up the cash."

"And I suppose he neglected to inform any of our team members about those underground tunnels?"

"That's correct sir. We discovered them after he disappeared."

"All right, Paisley. Call the search to a halt. I'm certain we won't find Mariska anywhere near here. Martray likely had her transported elsewhere. If we only knew where, we could use the MADS to rescue her."

"Yes sir." Paisley ended the call.

Aaric turned to the agents with him. "All right, back to home-base." And with that directive, all LSS agents used the MADS to return to Loradin and the LSS building.

The deployment arrived back at the LSS building just after two, as Harper and Bain had just entered the waiting room on the top floor.

Kinley notified Wilkins where to find them.

"Wilkins," Harper jumped to her feet and wrapped her arms around her husband. Bain too joined in the family hug, happy his father returned home safely.

Harper noticed the look on Wilkins face. "You didn't catch him, did you."

"No, we didn't."

Wilkins explained to Harper about the tunnels and the underground boat slip.

"Poor Mariska," Harper said, sinking down into the chair beside her.

"We'll find her Harper," Wilkins assured.

"No. No, I'm very afraid you won't. Not alive anyway."

"Try to be positive here, Harper..."

"You don't know Martray like I do. I seriously doubt he'll let her live we he discovers she isn't me," she said, tears beginning to fill her eyes.

"Maybe she'll fool him well enough."

"Well enough for what, Wil? For him to torture her. I doubt he wanted me as some sort of prize or prisoner to shuttle around with him. He likely planned to kill me. Do you think he'll do any different to her? Even if he doesn't find out she isn't me, she's as good as dead."

Wilkins and Bain looked at one another, unsure how to deal with the situation or Harper's current state of mind.

"Look," Wilkins knelt in front of her, taking her hands in his. "Why don't we just call it a day and head home."

Harper simply shook her head in agreement without uttering another word.

"Bain take your mom down to our Mod. I'll be right there. I just want to have a word with your grandfather."

"Sure, father." Bain and Harper walked to the elevator while Wilkins went back into his father's office. Aaric looked up to see him walk through the door.

"I'm taking Harper home. She's pretty upset that the mission was unsuccessful. Call me as soon as you hear anything about Mariska."

"Certainly, Son."

Wilkins was only seconds behind Harper and Bain. As soon as he reached the Mod they went straight home. Harper disappeared to the bathroom to take a long hot bath, while Bain and Wilkins stood in the kitchen and manned his com device. An hour later, the LSS call came through.

"We've found her," Aaric sighed sadly on the other end.

"Where?"

"It isn't good, Wil. She's dead. They shot her in the head and somehow dumped her body at one of the smaller unmanned coastal guard stations on the south side of Loradin."

Wilkins sighed, running a hand down his face.

"There's more," Aaric explained. "Martray left us a note, written in Mariska's own blood across her shirt."

"And..." Wilkins urged him due to the hesitation in his voice.

"It was a threat, against Harper, you, and the children. It said, 'I'll find them all.'"

Wilkins sighed heavily looking around the room to make certain Harper was still occupied elsewhere.

"This has to end, Father. I'll not have her worried about this. I don't want that message mentioned either."

"Understood, and, Wilkins, we *will* get this man. Make no mistake."

"Thanks." Wilkins ended the call and explained things to Bain who waited nearby.

"What are we going to do, Father?" Bain asked.

"Use every possible connection to find Martray before he finds us. I want this finished."

"I bet Uncle Finn knows someone who can help."

"You're probably right about that. Give him a call later when your mother isn't around and explain. See if he can meet up in the morning at the cafe near LSS headquarters."

"Yes sir, I'll do that as soon as I leave."

The next morning, it was Harper's day to keep Adda so fortunately she would be staying home. At the café, Wilkins, Finn, Bain, and Paisley, all discussed the need to capture Martray. Finn explained that Aaric had asked to see him that morning to discuss something, and as soon as he found out what, he would let them know and they would go from there.

Aaric stood behind his desk, peering out through the large window down over the city of Loradin toward the harbor. Finn and Paisley sat in chairs awaiting his orders.

"We need to form an alliance with the other governing members of Zanchier. That is, if we can find any of them to be uncorrupt."

Finn replied, "I am still in contact with a few of the original members of the rebellion. Most still very powerful men of influence. I'm certain that they would join with Loradin, as long as they know for sure that we are the good guys."

"Well then, Finn, see if you can get in touch with your contacts. We need to gather as many influential people as we can. See what you can do, and I'll get in touch with my contacts as well as the Loradin City council and LSS board of trustees today. Tomorrow morning, I would like to have a conference call with everyone about the current state of this impending war with the Scaithers. They've grown rather bold, and apparently now have ties here in Loradin to be able to leave Mariska's body on the shoreline. They should have never been able to get past the Coast guard. Not even if they had used MADS to enter the city. We should have been able to see the readings for the entry here in our AMD."

Finn looked confused. "AMD?" he asked.

"Activity Monitoring Department," Aaric answered. "We have equipment that allows us to see any and all activity coming into and going out of Loradin. If the signal is for another Matter Arranger Device that does not have a Loradin signature, then it should have pinged to alert us. If they used such a device to enter Loradin, then they likely had a Loradin made device, which means they have sympathizers here in the city. If they arrived by boat, then someone in the coast guard helped them. Either way, we have some problems to deal with in our fair city."

Paisley said, "Yes, it seems Martray's reach has now extended inside our borders."

"Yes," Aaric stated. "And that means no one is safe. Not even here."

Finn added, "Perhaps we should make sure that Harper and Wilkins children are safe. We might need to add more security detail to their watch."

"Yes, my grandchildren are of the utmost importance. I'll see to that personally. Let me know when you reach your contacts, Finn, and I'll give Kinley their contact information for the meeting. We'll convene tomorrow morning."

"Will do, also Aaric, there is a man in the Praxtingen market who used to be a part of the rebellion way back when I was just a lad. Bain has made friends with him. The man's name is Silus, and he seems to know quite a bit about some old equipment and hiding places used back then. He may be useful to us."

"Yes, quite. Paisley, run a background check on this Silus fellow." He then turned to Finn. "If he checks out then by all means bring him in tomorrow if you can." She nodded agreeably in reply as Finn stated, "Sure thing, Uncle." He and Paisley left Aaric's office to tend to their orders.

Raif Martray sat behind his desk, smug in the knowledge that they had gotten into Loradin and out again without any mishaps. He turned to Vonder Mortruff who was seated in one of the large leather chairs.

"I want Castor Briggs found and brought to me. That man cheated me out of a lot of rhedon. He needs to be taught a very important lesson. No one cheats me."

"I'll get the men on it ASAP."

"Also, you know that young man that Bain Brinley always used to hang around with. The one that Riglan always complains about. What was his name?"

"I think Riglan said it was Kreelie Rintel," Vonder replied. "What do you want with him?"

"To use him as bait. Perhaps even turn him to our side. That ought to put a thorn in Bain Brinley's side. Send Riglan to take care of that."

"The boys haven't always seen eye to eye. I don't know if Riglan could persuade this Kreelie boy to join us."

"Well, tell Riglan to be convincing," Martray said, a bit perturbed by the conversation.

"I'll see what we can do." Vonder left the office to find Riglan.

Raif Martray stood and looked out the large office window and down over the Mountains of Martanzia. He could just make out the tornadic activity in the Dustbowl region of Zanchier, getting its name due to the constant state of churning air. Raif grinned, knowing he had been responsible for the turbulent area which now existed because of the test of his powerful weapon of destruction. Then his smile turned to a frown as his brows knit together in anger as he remembered that fateful night, and Harper Brinley's actions. She had single-handedly destroyed his weapon and his plans. But, he always bounced back, and his plans for her and her family were well underway. Every bounty hunter around was looking for them, and now that he knew where they were, he could send his own thugs to take care of them all. He wouldn't need to spend another rhedon for her capture. And as for Castor Briggs, he would make the man pay tremendously for his betrayal and trickery.

Bain com-called Finn using the ear-piece technology as he rode through the darkening streets of Loradin. The lights of the city began to turn on as dusk settled on the horizon. Dusk was Bain's favorite time of day. Everything seemed to spring to life just as the sun began to set, streaking the sky with brilliant colors which was reflected on the surface of Everly Lake.

"Finn here."

"Uncle Finn,"

"Bain. What's up?"

"Father wanted to know if you had any contacts to help find Raif Martray. He said he wanted him found as quickly as possible. He's really worried about Mother."

"I know how he feels. I know a few people. Your grandfather wants me to contact them anyway to form an alliance. I'll get on that as soon as we finish talking. Why don't you swing by my place, and we can talk more?"

"Great. I'll be there in five minutes."

"Okay, see you then."

Bain arrived as predicted, and he and Finn went out to sit on the balcony overlooking the darkening city of Loradin as the sun dipped below the water's edge.

"I could have just called Wilkins you know," Finn stated, handing Bain a beverage.

Bain shook his head as he took a sip of the cool liquid. "Mother might get curious. He doesn't want to involve her. She's already upset about Mariska's death, and the fact that Martray is still at large. Besides, I wanted to talk to you about something. I've decided to join the field agents. I'm definitely not needed in the tech department."

"Have you spoken to your grandfather about that?"

"Not yet, but I will tonight after I leave here."

"What about your Mother? How do you think she is going to take that news?"

"I don't know, but I can't just hang around the LSS building all day doing nothing. They have plenty of technological geniuses. I feel like I'm not really contributing. Besides, the agents see a lot more action. I'm bored out of my mind already and I only started four months ago. Anyway, it's my decision."

Finn smiled at his statement. "That's true, it is your decision. But just keep in mind that a highly trained agent, with years of experience died today. And because of that, your mother is going to blow a gasket."

"I can deal with mother." Bain smiled. "Besides, she works for the LSS too, doing the same type of work, so she can't really say much."

Finn chuckled, "You want to make a bet on that?"

Bain laughed along with Finn. "No."

Finn said, "Listen, your grandfather also wanted me to speak with Silus about his past with the resistance. You want to join me tomorrow while I speak to him? It might help since you and he are friends."

"Sure. I haven't talked with Silus since mom went all gangster on Castor Briggs." Bain smiled at the memory.

"Yeah." Finn smiled. Then his face became more serious. "If I had only let her shoot the man we wouldn't have lost Mariska."

"It's hard to know who to trust, Uncle Finn."

"You have no idea how true that is kid," Finn patted him on the shoulder. "Speaking of people you can trust, have you spoken to your friend Kreelie lately about coming to Loradin and working for the LSS?"

Bain shook his head no. "It's been several weeks since we last talked. He said he was juggling some life decisions and he just wasn't sure what he was going to do yet."

"What kind of decisions?"

Bain shrugged. "He didn't say. It's not like Kreelie to keep anything from me. We always told each other everything. Now, since I've moved here to Loradin, it seems like we're growing apart."

"Distance has a way of doing that to people. You should call him soon."

"Yeah, I think I will."

Finn and Bain chatted a bit longer while Bain finished his beverage. Bain soon left and minutes later pulled up to his apartment building. He parked the Bi-Mod, entered his apartment, and collapsed on the sofa. He called his grandfather to ask about joining the field agents, to which he got a yes but only if Harper signed off on it. Bain decided to leave discussing that with his mother for tomorrow. After hanging up with his grandfather Aaric, he called Kreelie, who didn't pick up the call. Bain sighed, feeling like he was losing his best friend. He kept his com device close while he got ready for bed, just in case Kreelie called back. Bain soon fell asleep as he stared at the ceiling of his quiet room, wondering if things were all right with Kreelie.

Chapter 12

Misunderstood

Doctor Patrice Barrister smiled as she watched with delight at the connection between young Wynne Brinley and the fledgling Kabihanxu.

"Excellent job Wynne," she stated, as Wynne walked around the young firebird, petting, and playing with the large creature.

The firebird cooed and squawked in response to Wynne's movements. She giggled and wrapped her arms around the bird's neck as it nuzzled her back with its head and beak. The two of them stood looking at each other for a moment when Wynne asked, "Are you certain?"

The bird knelt down as Wynne slung her leg across its back at the base of its neck, drawing the attention of those working nearby.

Patrice reacted quickly. "Wynne," she squealed, "what are you doing?"

"Roamey wishes to go for a walk. Actually, he wants to fly but there is no room in his cage."

"But why are you on his back?"

"He asked me to go with him. Can't we let him out of the cage, just for a little while? All of his down has been shed and his flight feathers have now grown in. He'll never learn to fly otherwise."

"I don't know. I suppose you're right about his learning to fly, but you cannot ride him while he learns. Perhaps afterward if he doesn't fly off and not return."

"All right." Wynne leaned over and whispered to the bird before climbing down.

Patrice nervously stated, "I'm not so sure this is such a good idea, releasing him so close to the city."

"He won't harm anyone. I instructed him to be cautious of the people and the buildings. I told him that if he wishes to be daring to fly out over the lake."

Patrice looked at her, unsure the bird would obey. She looked at the workers as she readied to unlock the gate to the cage. "Swing the gates open quickly and stand back." She then looked at Wynne. "Are you certain about this?"

"Yes. It will be fine, Doctor Barrister."

Patrice shook her head, hoping that she didn't live to regret letting this natural predator loose on the city of Loradin. She breathed deeply and let out a slow breath. She unlocked the lock, and the workers quickly opened the gates. The young firebird trotted through, flinging his head around, and stretching his wings and flapping them. The wind from its powerful wings stirred the dust on the ground and ruffled their hair and clothing.

It pranced about happily, turning toward the water, and taking off at a run toward the docks. It flapped its wings and jumped into the air just over the water's edge. The young bird flew high into the sky, twisting and turning in the air, excitedly expelling small, short bursts of fire as it learned to fly and belch fire from deep within its chest.

Patrice and the others jumped slightly at the first expulsion, everyone except Wynne, who laughed and clapped happily for her young firebird friend. Roamey screeched loudly, drawing the attention of not only the LARS workers and students, but anyone within the vicinity of the institute. Many looked to the skies as to the reason for the noise. Upon seeing the firebird soaring over LARS, the LSS office and the coast guard began receiving many calls.

Two blocks away at the Bayview Apartments, Bain heard the screech and peered out his apartment window just in time to see the Kabihanxu take flight. He knew Wynne had been interacting with the creature. It must have gotten loose from its cage. He hurriedly gathered his jacket and ran out the door.

Roamey landed again, prancing excitedly around Wynne. He knelt low to allow her to climb upon his back. She leaped up and grabbed tightly around his neck, locking her fingers around his thick feathers. He took to the air again and the two of them soared across Everly Lake, taking to the sky higher and higher until the clouds surrounded them.

Wynne's heart was so full of joy she felt she would explode. She never imagined her talents, or gifts as Dr. Patrice called them, would take her to such heights, literally. She was grateful for her unique abilities to talk to creatures. It allowed her to do things very few others could.

She and Roamey flew through the sky as she peered down at the scene below her. Zanchier was such a beautiful place, especially from her view on the back of the Kabihanxu. She remembered the airship flight they had taken a few months back. But that could not compare to the sensations she felt now. The sun's rays warmed her skin, a contrast to the cool air that also blew against her as they coasted through the sky. The puffy white clouds felt like a light misty rain against her flesh. As they flew in and out of clouds, the world below changed scenery every so often. She could see for miles and miles. The mountains of Carpasia to the east looked monstrous compared to the Bakrashan and Xantifal mountains far off to the west, which looked like small ant-hills at this distance. The tall glistening buildings of Loradin reflected sunlight and looked like jewels as the taller buildings were reflected in the glasslike surface of the water that surrounded the island.

She didn't want to return to the institute, but she decided that they should. "All right, Roamey. This is loads of fun, but Dr. Patrice will be worried. We need to return to LARS now."

Roamey squawked his reply and turned back toward the institute, flying lower as they went. When Wynne and Roamey got closer to the institute she saw all manner of Mods and military type uniforms on the ground. Dr. Patrice was talking excitedly to these uniformed, military people, and pushing at the guns they had in their hands, aimed at Wynne and Roamey. They landed on the platform of the institutes back fenced area and Roamey squawked loudly making those with the weapons a bit jumpy. However, when they saw the young girl on the firebird's back they all dropped their weapons a bit and simply stared, mouths gaping open in shock. Wynne could hear Dr. Patrice yelling loudly in protest to one tall, broad-shouldered man in a coastal uniform.

"You idiot! Can't you see one of my students on the Kabihanxu's back?"

"Yes ma'am, *I can*. And why may I ask is she doing that? Don't you people know how dangerous those animals are? What are you teaching these kids here anyway?" the tall, muscular, military man yelled back. He watched cautiously as Wynne dismounted the bird and made her way toward him and the doctor.

Wynne saw Bain standing off to the side, smiling broadly at her. "Bain," she said excitedly and raced over to hug him. The two of them walked toward Doctor Patrice.

Wynne stopped in front of the coast guard captain and simply said, "Hello."

The man looked down at her with a serious and slightly confused look on his face. "Just what exactly were you doing on the back of that thing?" he asked her, pointing at Roamey.

"Flying of course," she answered confused, looking up at Bain as if she were supposed to answer differently.

The man shifted his weight and replied. "I can see that, young lady. What made you think you should ride him?"

Patrice interrupted, "I've been trying to tell you, Captain. My students are a very gifted bunch of children who can communicate with animals."

The captain looked back and forth between the hot-headed, yet rather attractive doctor who stood glaring at him with her arms folded over her chest, and the young, innocent, smiling young girl who stood beaming up at him.

"He's quite harmless," Wynne stated. "To answer your question, Sir, Roamey asked me to fly with him. He's just been learning to fly. Roamey's been caged in this pen since he was a hatchling." She motioned to the large, fenced area.

The captain looked around at the many caged animals at the institute. *Wait, did she say it asked her to fly with it?* he wondered, very confused.

"He should still be caged. Not that a cage would stop him should he want to break free. He does breathe fire after-all and could likely melt that fence without any problems."

"Yes, he's just learned that too! But he knows he's caged for his own good and that it is only temporary," Wynne stated proudly. She turned to her brother. "You should have seen it Bain. Roamey was brilliant!" She turned to look at the captain. Wynne watched the different emotions flit across the man's face as he looked back and forth between the three of them. The two smiling teenagers and the stern looking doctor. The Captain's attention was drawn upward behind them, and his face grew concerned. His gun quickly lifted above their heads and his stance was one of defense. They all turned to see Roamey walking up to them. He stretched out his beak to Wynne just as she turned and the two of them nuzzled one another.

The captain never lowered his weapon, but he watched in amazement and confusion at the two unlikely friends before him.

He yelled to his men. "Stand down. No one fires!"

His handful of men lowered their guns, but never relaxed their stances, keeping both hands planted firmly on their weapons. They all watched in amazement at the interaction of the very young girl and the very large juvenile bird.

Dr. Patrice turned to Wynne. "Wynne, perhaps it's time to put Roamey back in his cage. I think we've had enough excitement for one day."

"Yes ma'am. Goodbye Captain." Wynne grinned brightly at the both of them, and she and Bain walked Roamey back inside his cage. Wynne went about giving him a special treat and interacting with him, as Bain also got some attention from the playful juvenile bird. His confidence unwavering only because Wynne was with him.

The captain lowered his weapon slowly as he watched the three young beings. He noticed how they interacted, as though the creature could understand what the young girl said to it.

Patrice broke through his musings, realizing what he was likely wondering. "Yes, Captain, the firebird *can* understand Wynne, and she *it*."

He turned to her. "How is that possible? I've never seen or heard of anyone capable of this."

Patrice watched Wynne, Bain, and Roamey playing in the cage. "I believe there has always been those who were given this gift. In our society, we look for a child's talent early. If they don't display one then they are deemed talentless, cast into lower society life, and given the lowest of all positions. However, not everyone who is talentless has this gift, but I have found several young people who do."

"Do all the kids I see out here playing and interacting with these creatures have this same gift?"

"Yes. Although, none are as strongly connected to their abilities as young Wynne. She is the only one so far who the young Kabihanxu has bonded with. I believe their connection is unique."

"So she only connects with the firebird?" the captain asked, trying to grasp this new knowledge.

"No. Wynne can connect with all the creatures. And when she is around, they tend to follow her more so than they do the others. It's quite remarkable to watch. It's as if they are all drawn to her. But she is drawn more to Roamey."

"Do you name all the creatures you keep here?"

Patrice turned to him and stiffly grinned. "No. I don't name them. The children do. Especially Wynne. Our purpose here at the institute is to rehabilitate injured animals and return them to the wild. The workers try not to get to attached. But these telepathic children form unbreakable bonds with these creatures. It simply can't be helped."

"Doc, I think I need to know more about what you do here. Especially since it might pose problems with Loradin security. How did we never know about what goes on here before?"

"Well, Captain, no one has ever asked. Besides, we've never released anything this large this close to the city. We usually return them to wherever it is we found them. But, since I initiated this program with the gifted children we have been holding onto the creatures a bit longer. I do plan to take the children out into the forests and mountains one day soon to see if the interaction with wild creatures would be the same as it is here."

"When you do that, give me a call. You and the children may need some protection out there."

"I'll keep that in mind, Captain," Patrice stated as they walked toward the now caged Roamey.

"Donner, ma'am. Captain Donner."

"Of course, Captain Donner. I appreciate your offer, and although I doubt we will need your protection however, I may take you up on that."

"Ma'am," he said, nodding before turning to take his leave. The other guards following him out of the institute. As they were leaving the premises, Finn and Paisley were arriving from the LSS.

Finn knew that Wynne was in some sort of special program here at LARS, but nothing prepared him for what he saw when he arrived.

"Wynne, Bain! You two get out of that cage before you get hurt!"

Dr. Patrice approached. "They're fine, sir, I assure you."

"You must be Patrice Barrister," Finn stated, a bit irritated.

"Yes. And you are?" she asked, with the same irritability.

"Finn Mobley, and this is my wife Paisley." Paisley nodded and smiled at the doctor.

Just then, Wynne yelled, "Uncle Finn, Aunt Paisley!" She ran toward them as Bain followed behind.

Finn bent down and hugged Wynne. Paisley did the same.

Wynne proudly announced to Doctor Barrister, "This is my aunt and uncle. Finn and Paisley Mobley." Wynne turned to Finn excitedly and filled him in on what had happened that day. Finn wasn't too sure he liked what he heard and often glanced toward Patrice Barrister with looks of annoyance.

When Wynne had finished her story, Patrice said, "Wynne, why don't you and the other children go inside now and start your reading lessons. I'll be in shortly."

"Yes Ma'am. Goodbye Bain, goodbye Uncle Finn, Aunt Paisley," she waved as she ran off, reaching the other children who all quickly gathered around her and excitedly questioned her about her earlier flight.

"Doctor Barrister, I don't know exactly what sort of academy you're running here, but if anything happens to my niece you'll have me to answer to," Finn seethed.

"Mr. Mobely," Patrice answered irritably, "Wynne is quite safe I assure you. And as far as *'what sort of academy I'm running here'*, well, I've been doing it for years, and quite successfully I might add. All without yours or anyone else's input. The children in my care and tutelage are quite safe. More so then they would have been without my academy since they would have likely been sent to the mines or harvest fields. I have had quite enough already this morning from overbearing, musclebound men bearing weapons. Now, *if* you'll excuse me, I have an institute to run. Bain." She nodded at him, before turning on her heels and marching inside the institute.

Finn stated as he watched her go, "Well, she's a hothead."

Bain laughed. "Uncle Finn, you did chew her out for no reason. Wynne's doing really well here. Doctor Barrister is giving her the chance to use her gifts."

"I wasn't aware she had a gift?" Finn stated.

Bain shrugged. "I guess with everything going on lately, Mother just hasn't had a chance to fill you in."

"I haven't exactly tried talking to Harper lately either. You're right, we all have been very busy. I suppose I owe Doctor Barrister an apology for the misunderstanding."

Paisley smiled, "I'd say you owe her a big one."

Finn smiled at her. "Later. I'll not interfere with her day anymore. But I want some answers," he said turning to Bain. "Wynne can talk with animals, and she rides Kabihanxus?"

He and Paisley listened intently as Bain described Wynne's abilities while they left the LARS building and mounted their Bi-Mods.

Finn asked, "Bain, we're heading over to the Praxtingen Market to speak with Silus. You have time for that right now?"

"Sure do Uncle Finn. I'll see you there." With that, Bain's Bi-mod roared to life, and he took off toward Praxtingen, followed by Finn and Paisley.

Chapter 13

Wars and Rumors of War

"Silus!" Bain yelled and waved to the large man from across the street as he approached the booth.

"Bain, nice to see you. What brings you out this way today?" Silus asked.

Bain turned to watch Finn and Paisley approach Silus's booth. "Uncle Finn wanted to speak with you, and I decided to tag along."

"Is that so?" Silus asked curiously. "What about exactly?"

Finn stopped in front of Silus and shook the man's hand. "Silus." Finn nodded hello.

"Mr. Mobely," Silus returned.

"Finn will do," he replied. "this is my wife Paisley."

"Hello," Silus said taking her offered hand.

Paisley smiled brightly at him.

Finn began. "Silus, is there somewhere a bit more private that we could talk?"

Silus looked around at the people milling about. "Sure, right this way," he said, motioning behind his table. "There's a bit of a quiet area over here where I take my lunch sometimes, or just try to get out of the heat of the day." He turned the closed sign around which hung from his booth and led them to a small, shady spot where a few chairs and a table sat. He motioned for them to have a seat.

Finn got right to the point. "Silus, the LSS would like to recruit you. We believe that the small wars that have been plaguing Zanchier for the last several years are increasing in frequency, and that a large-scale battle is about to take place. Especially since Loradin's boarders have been breached by the Scaithers."

"Scaithers? Here?" Silus said disbelieving.

"Unfortunately, yes."

"That's probably all my families fault," Bain replied.

Finn looked up at the young man who leaned against a railing. "They were bound to try and take over Loradin too eventually."

Everyone nodded in agreement. Silus asked, "What does that have to do with me?"

Finn answered, "I know you were in the resistance back when you were younger. I also know that you know about things that few others do. Things that may swing this fight in our favor. Maybe Paisley can explain better. She's been with the LSS a lot longer than I have."

Paisley began. "The Zanchier government, specifically Loradin, has tried to stay neutral in the mining wars. Some Loradians; the social elitists and wealthy land barons; have been involved in the mining wars for years with the Martanzians. The LSS, Loradin Secret Society, was formed many years ago to protect the people of Loradin and Praxtingen from the repercussions that these battles over the mines would cause. Now however, it seems that all of Zanchier is geared up and ready to go to war with one another. Loradin has been attacked by the Scaithers, whom we believe to be behind all the war mongering to begin with. There is a man, Raif Martray, who we believe is controlling the Zanchieths. He somehow has control of some very powerful people, even some high up on the council, and we believe he is pulling all the strings. We need to prepare for an eminent attack. Just the fact that they were able to penetrate our boarders without detection is scary enough."

Silus listened intently, then said, "Well, if there is anything I can do to protect Praxtingen and Loradin, I'll do my part. What do you need from me exactly?"

Finn spoke up, "Uncle, our boss, would like your expertise on the hidden communications room and the equipment that you say should still be there. We may be able to use that to our advantage."

"You got it. When do you want to go check out the caves?"

"Whenever is best for you."

"All right then. Meet me back here at the market this evening around 4 p.m. That should give us time to check things out before it gets too late."

They all shook hands in agreement, left Silus to his booth, and returned to LSS headquarters.

Bain, Finn, and Paisley entered the LSS building, passing through the hallways of the tech department and saying their good mornings to their colleagues. Bain looked up to see Harper headed his way, a thunderous look plastered on her face. Finn offered him an apologetic look and he and Paisley ducked out of the way and continued on to their destination.

"Mother," Bain smiled tightly as he came to a halt, ready to protest the certain onslaught.

"How could you, Bain?"

"How could I what?"

"You know what. Join the field agents. You *know* how dangerous it is."

"Yes Ma'am, I do. But I also know I'm going crazy doing nothing here."

"What about the tech department?"

"Really? You know that the brain-train that is Winnie, Cranston, and Maubrey, has absolutely *no* need of me."

"I'm sure your grandfather Aaric could find something else for you to do?"

"This *is* something else. You do the same type of work, Mother."

"Yes, but that is different."

"How? Why is it okay for you when you still have Wynne and Adda to raise, to risk your life and it isn't okay for me?"

Harper stood there looking at her grown up son. "I just don't want to lose you, Bain."

"You won't Mother. You just have to trust in my abilities. Besides, we're fighting for the good guys here. The Creator will protect me."

Harper had started talking to the Creator herself lately, but she had no idea Bain believed. She really didn't know her children at all. This realization pained her even more. She knew she had no right to tell him how to live his life. He had turned into a man all those years without her.

"Just promise me that you'll be careful and not take any unnecessary chances. The difference between the other agents and us is that we are being hunted by Raif Martray, and possibly a slew of bounty hunters as well. You have to be on alert all the time."

"I know, Mother. I promise. I realized that you weren't just being overprotective when Castor Briggs appeared. I'll watch out for myself, and Seadon and Wynne whenever possible. Even little Adda, but I suspect she will be taken care of by the rest of the family."

"Yes, she will. But so will Seadon and Wynne. You just make sure you look after yourself. And don't get angry with me should you find me trailing behind you."

"I promise. As long as you understand that I have to do what I feel I need too?" Bain looked at her. He had missed his parents so much for so long. Suddenly having them back in his life as an apprenticing adult was strange, but he would enjoy it as much as possible. Even his mother's somewhat overbearing yet understandably protective nature. He decided he would try to never take that for granted.

Harper sighed heavily and grinned, "Deal." She smiled at her sixteen-year-old son who seemed much older due to his maturity. She hugged him as they took the elevator up to the top-level offices in search of Wilkins. She locked her arm in his for the remainder of the elevator ride.

When they stepped off the elevator and walked to Aaric's office, Finn and Paisley were already there speaking to Aaric and Wilkins about the arrangement with Silus.

"Great news," Aaric replied. "We can use all the help we can get. What about your contacts in Martanzia Finn? Are they still willing to fight for the new resistance?"

"I com-called him last night. He's in. He just wants to check with some of his other contacts first to be certain of their allegiances. He did say that the Zanchieth council will be meeting the day after tomorrow and that they've called all the governing members to gather for talks concerning the rumors of war."

"Hmm…I wonder why we haven't been notified of this," Aaric pondered.

"I think he said it was just recently decided. Perhaps they haven't had time to alert you yet?"

"Perhaps. Or maybe our mole is closer than we think. Someone had to disable the alert system that surrounds the island and tell them where to drop Mariska's body. The entire system doesn't shut down all at once, only smaller areas between coastguard buildings. So, I think we need to look into the people who work at the two buildings near where she was found and those in charge over those areas."

Wilkins stood up. "I'll see to that."

"Great, thank you Wil." Aaric turned back to Finn. "When do you think you'll hear from your Martanzian contacts again?"

Zanchier Book 2: Uprising

"Should be some time this morning." Finn answered, as Aaric thoughtfully shook his head in reply.

Harper asked, "Has anyone checked on Seadon lately?"

Aaric answered her with, "The team watches the monitors at all hours of the night. Even while he sleeps. There has been nothing out of the ordinary as of yet."

"And Wynne?"

"Dr. Barrister was a bit hesitant about the cameras when we called her, seeing as how they already have security cameras in place. She did however allow us to link into her system and watch over Wynne that way. Plus, she assured us that they monitor everyone who comes and goes around the institute because of the animals possibly being a danger to anyone unfamiliar with them."

Finn turned to Harper. "I hear Wynne has quite the gift. She caused a bit of a stir this morning out at the institute. Had the coastal guard and local Policing Authority show up armed to the teeth."

Harper looked surprised. "What happened, and why wasn't I told earlier?"

Bain chuckled, "Whoa, Mother, slow down. It wasn't a big deal."

As he explained to her what happened, she slumped into a nearby chair.

"I knew she could communicate with them, but to fly on the back of a Kabihanxu is another thing entirely. What if she falls off and gets hurt, or she can't control the thing and it takes off with her."

"But *she can* control it Mother. It listens to everything she says. Almost like *she's* its mother or something. I saw her land with the firebird. It was totally cool. You should have seen the faces of all the military personnel, it was a hoot," Bain said, laughing a bit at the earlier memory and the commotion the fledgling and Wynne had caused.

"I sort of saw them land, although I didn't realize Wynne was riding it," Finn replied. "That Dr. Barrister sure is a feisty one. I'm sure Wynne is in good hands."

Paisley laughed. "She has to be feisty with all you overbearing men butting in and chewing her out."

Wilkins knelt down beside Harper, "We know Wynne is safe. She'll be just fine. I pity anyone who tries to mess with her. I've seen the way that firebird acts when she is around.

It's totally smitten with her. And I figure, if it wanted to break loose, that cage wouldn't be able to hold it."

Harper grinned up at her husband's attempt to lighten her mood. "All right. I'm fine. I'm not going to think about it. Besides, I have enough to worry about with Raif Martray still on the loose."

Aaric replied, "Whom we are using all our resources to find, Harper. We *will* eventually catch him. Along with that spineless bounty hunter Castor Briggs."

Finn looked at Aaric. "You can leave Cass to me. I'm pretty sure I know where to find him."

"Fine. Now, as for the meeting of the governors and council members day after tomorrow, how many of you would like to sit in on the meeting?"

Harper shivered. "I would if it weren't for seeing Raif Martray there. I promise you he'll be close. He has to have his hands in the pockets of some pretty influential people."

Finn put in, "That is a fact. My contacts in Martanzia say that Raif Martray and Vonder Mortruff run the city like their own personal playground. And, they have all the Policing Authorities in their pockets as well."

This got Bain's attention. "Are you sure about that, Uncle Finn? Kreelie's dad runs the Everly Sound division. I never thought of Mr. Rintel being a dirty cop."

"Just because the Policing Authority is in his pocket, doesn't mean everyone who works for the authority is. Your friend's dad could be clean and honest."

Bain's mind became a whirlwind of questions as he thought about his friend and them growing up together. He tried to remember if he ever thought he saw or heard anything shady when listening to Mr. Rintel speak. Nothing came to mind. Of course, no one really knew how long Raif Martray had been in power.

Seadon loved training at the Praxtingen Airship Academy. It was much more intensive than the Loradin Secondary Academy. The first few days in classes were a little hard, until the older kids realized he wasn't going to be bullied.

Zanchier Book 2: Uprising

Now, they respected him as an equal, even though he was much younger than most everyone else. Today they would train on an actual airship, learning different things about their operations.

He and the other trainees watched as Captain Matt Easton steered the massive airship through the sky and out over Everly Lake. Today, they were working on evasive maneuvers and how to fend off a Kabihanxu attack.

Captain Easton turned to address the crowd. "Now, I want everyone to notice the lever located to the left of the controls, just beneath the edge of the control board. This lever is attached to a cooling chamber filled with CO_2. Can anyone tell me what CO_2 is?"

Seadon raised his hand.

"Yes Seadon."

"CO_2, commonly known as Carbon Dioxide is used to extinguish fires by dispelling Oxygen which feeds fire."

"Correct, Seadon," Captain Easton grinned. "Now, can anyone else tell me why we would keep CO_2 on board an airship?"

Another student answered, "In case the ship catches fire. It may prevent a crash."

"Yes, very good. That is one likely answer, but there is another reason. Anyone else?"

Seadon answered again. "In case we encounter any Kabihanxu's?"

"Precisely. You see, the lever here can be pushed or pulled. It works in both the forward and the aft positions. If there is a fire on board an airship, you pull the lever toward you, which will release the valve shooting CO_2 to the affected area within the ship's interior. If you push it away, toward the shell of the ship, it will release a valve to the outside of the ship, putting out any fires that take place outside. It also has a booster button which will allow the captain or co-captain to disperse the CO_2 to an operator at the gunners position to spray any attacking firebirds. One blast with the CO_2 gun and it will head for the hills. However, using the CO_2 in this fashion will run your supply low very quickly, so be very sure you're under attack before wasting it on firebirds, and use as little as possible."

Everyone took turns using the lever and the buttons to switch to the gunner position. They were even allowed to shoot the gun to see how it worked and how far it traveled. Seadon was shocked to realize it shot out a good distance.

Captain Easton gave each student a chance to steer the ship, as did the co-captain. People took turns sitting in each chair to see to the duties of each one.

Seadon was the last to steer the ship because Captain Easton wanted to train him to land the airship.

"Steady now, Seadon. Make sure your bubble is in line with the center of the compass so that you land straight. Landing too far to one side may result in the airship tipping over. We don't want that, now do we?"

"No sir," Seadon answered, cautiously watching the instruments on the dash.

"Slowly release the thrusters for the landing now. Good, good. Now hold her steady."

Seadon did as told, and the airship landed with a small thud.

"Well done, Seadon." The captain slapped him on the shoulder, nearly knocking him into the steering wheel.

The captain turned to the rest of the class. "Tomorrow we will attempt taking off and landing in the simulators. Everyone have a good day, class dismissed. Seadon, may I speak with you a moment?"

"Certainly, Captain sir."

"Seadon, I'm quite impressed with your ability to learn the ship so quickly. You excel far beyond your years."

"Well, Sir, it's all I've ever wanted to do."

"Even still, you have a gift for flying. I'm curious to see where it takes you. I'll be watching your career with much interest."

"Yes sir. Thank you, Sir." Seadon smiled to himself as he walked off the ship headed to his next class. Which, believe it or not, was animal behaviors. He actually liked the class now that he had gotten to see and touch a few of the animals they studied. Besides, he figured it might be a good idea to know about anything that might, or could, attack an airship.

Chapter 14

A Country Divided

Bain, Finn, Paisley, Wilkins, and Harper, all met with Silus at the Praxtingen Market at 4 p.m. that afternoon as planned. From there Silus took them to Discovery Falls.

Bain asked once they had arrived, "Why is it called Discovery Falls, Silus?"

"Well, we couldn't name it hidden cave falls, because someone might hear that and realize there was something to find down there," he said, pointing to the falls before them.

"Make sense," Bain replied.

"Yes, I suppose it wouldn't do any good to have a hidden base and then tell everyone that it was there," Wilkins put in.

They all walked up the west side of the falls near the road that disappeared into the forest. Silus pulled back a curtain of thick, green, trailing vines to reveal a rock-facing. He pushed on a smaller rock, and it slid inward, releasing a deep clicking sound as the rock-facing in front of them moved ever so slightly. Silus pushed on the rock, and it slung inward into a dark passageway. He pulled out his torchlight and stepped inside, followed by the others.

Bain smiled, "This is a lot easier than swimming into the cave."

Silus laughed, "Maybe so, but not nearly as fun, eh?"

"I don't know about that," Bain replied. "A secret passage through rock is pretty cool stuff."

They followed Silus a little further until he stopped in front of a door. He pulled a set of keys from his pocket, inserted one into the lock, turned it jiggling the lock some, and then the door clicked. He smiled and pushed open the door.

"I wasn't sure that lock would work after all these years. Especially with the moisture the falls create," Silus said with relief. He walked inside, fumbled with a generator, flipped a few switches, and the lights inside the room blinked to life. Silus then went over to a dashboard filled with switches, buttons, and lights, pushed a few of them and the switchboard lit up, blinking and flashing. Gages began to twitch, and static could be heard coming from a handheld radio hanging from the switchboard.

Wilkins asked first, "What is all of this?"

Silus grinned. "Communications between hidden towers, all over Zanchier. This stuff is ancient, far older than me even, but it still seems like it wants to work. Let's hope it does. We'll be able to communicate with others all over Zanchier on hidden frequencies. No one uses this technology anymore, so they'll never hear us."

Paisley looked around the room appreciatively, leaning down to look at things and dusting off equipment with a swipe of her hand. "That is good news, Silus. We'll need all the help we can get. I feel Loradin might be the underdog in this potential war we face. Let's hope this equipment gives us an edge."

"I believe it will. It will at least allow us to hide should the need arise. Plus, there are other rooms down here. Very large ones. Come this way, I'll give you a tour."

Paisley asked as they walked, "I assume it all runs off the power of the falls?"

"You assume correctly. Might as well use what the Creator supplied, right?" He smiled broadly.

Paisley smiled at his reply.

Silus led them through a series of doors. Each one opening onto a larger room. The first room held old fold out bunks with dingy, dusty mattresses. There was also large locker-type cabinets with blankets, and other necessary items. Some too old to be of use, but others still in good condition. The next room was a galley kitchen stocked with everything someone would need to whip up large meals to feed troops. The last room they came to was very large with another huge generator to light the many hanging fixtures. The area was massive.

Harper had to ask, "What is a room like this used for?"

Silus smiled. "Let me just show you. He walked over to an empty flat wall and pulled a large lever downward and locked it into place near the floor. There was a deep clicking sound, and light began to filter through as the top of the wall began to lay open, bringing the grass and part of the road inside with it. It slowly touched down on the floor, revealing a ramp that led up and out.

Wilkins harrumphed. "When Bain and I explored this area last week I wondered why a road would just suddenly end at the forest line. This makes perfect sense, although I never would have guessed that this was why. Impressive construction."

"Yeah it is. The old-timers were smart, problem-solving men. They could figure out just about anything. Necessity being the mother of invention and all," Silus said, smiling broadly. "My dad helped to build this escape gate. Of course, you have to be a good bit ahead of the enemy to not be seen. The gate is a bit slow and sluggish."

Bain grinned, "I bet Winnie, Cranston, and Maubrey could have that thing swishing open and closed quicker than you could blink."

"True," Paisley replied. "Those three can make anything work better."

Finn put in, "Kamsten might could help with that as well."

"Well, Silus. Any more impressive old tech or hideouts you'd like to show us?" Wilkins asked.

"This is about all of it. I'll show you a few more escape passages should anything happen down here, and you need to get out. Follow me." He switched off lights and turned off the generators as they went from room to room. He showed them four other passages to exit the hidden cave rooms beneath Discovery Falls. One that led into the forest from the largest room. One that led to the other side of the falls on top, where Wilkins, Bain, Harper, and the kids exited on their picnic, branching off into the cave where Bain entered the first time he came alone. One that actually led into the water just behind the falls, and one more that led deep into the back of the cavern, beneath the river that fed the falls.

"We won't walk that one seeing as how it goes for a few miles into the forest. It comes out near the top of the Carpasian Mountains through a small hidden bunker that exits out into the forest," Silus explained. "Years ago, there was a small village of homes built into the tree tops up there that only a few people knew about. It could house several hundred people between all the dwellings built in the trees, hidden within the large branches, and camouflaged beneath so no one would know they existed. Of course, I don't know how sturdy those houses still are. It's been many years since those were constructed."

Finn stated, "It warrants taking a look. We might need a place like that to hide. Even if it's just to help the citizens of Zanchier to have a safe place from the fighting."

"Well, if you're all up to the walk, we can do it," Silus responded. "But I tell you it'll be getting dark soon and the Kabihanxus' and Pagorinxes do live up that way. We would be at a disadvantage."

"True," Finn stated. How about we return tomorrow? Would that be all right with you, Silus?"

"Sure. Missing a market day isn't going to hurt me none. Shall we say 8 a.m. by the hidden vine passage?"

"Sounds like a plan," Finn replied. "Everyone else good with that?"

They all replied yes or agreed with a shake of their heads.

"See you in the morning, Silus," Finn replied. Everyone said their goodbyes and left, headed for home now that it was growing late. Bain decided that since he was so close to the Praxtingen Airship Academy that he would go see Seadon. He hadn't talked to his brother in a week and was curious as to how things were going. As he pulled up to the academy, it was nearing dinnertime. Bain com-called Seadon to see where he was and if he could join him for dinner. As Bain parked the Bi-Mod and walked toward the building, Seadon appeared, smiling brightly.

"Bain, good to see you. What brings you up this way?"

Bain smiled at his brother, slinging his arm across his shoulder. "Have I got some things to tell you about. I hope you get a long dinner."

"Dinner lasts for hours. We get as long as we want since classes are over."

"Great. Let's go stuff our faces and chat."

Seadon and Bain walked into the academy café as Bain told Seadon everything that had been going on lately. He started with Castor Briggs, Harper nearly taking his head off, Mariska being murdered, Wynne riding the Kabihanxu, his new appointment with the field agents, the hidden rooms at the falls, treehouses they were to explore tomorrow, and the council meeting in a few days. They spent the next hour catching up with one another.

The next morning, everyone met at the hidden entrance beneath Discovery Falls. They walked the long dark passage, only lit by their torchlights. Nearly an hour later, they exited into a small bunker that had a door that opened up into the surrounding forest. The outside hidden to look like the forest around it. Finn stepped out first, heavily armed against any Kabihanxu or Pagorinxes that might be lurking nearby. With the area being secure, they all stepped out and followed Silus through the woods until he soon came to a stop.

"Look up everyone. See anything?"

Everyone peered into the large, tall trees, but could see nothing.

"This way," Silus waved them on. He soon stopped at a massively wide tree. He pulled on a knot in the tree and a part of the tree slid open, revealing a doorway and a circular staircase that went up through the center of the tree.

"This tree is fabricated," Harper replied, amazed.

"Yes. There was no way to hollow out a real tree like this and it survive, so my father and many other men engineered this tree to look as real as the others. There are several other ways to get into the treetops. Hidden rope ladders, pulley systems, and rope bridges, that pull into place when needed but this is the easiest way for those who are physically impaired, especially the elderly. There's even a small lifting platform in the staircase center here that works with pulleys.

It has to be operated by several men though, depending on how heavy the person in the center is. It's operated from the top, lifted and lowered."

Harper marveled at the construction. "This is amazing, Silus. Your father was a truly brilliant craftsman."

"Thanks, but it wasn't all him. He did design it though."

The twisting staircase rose to over sixty feet in the air, stopping at a platform at the top. The top of the tree platform was open to all directions with thick poles holding the top of the tree to the rest of the trunk. There were rope bridges leading in six directions from the platform out to other treehouses. And further rope bridges, all hidden in the canopies branching out to other treehouses. It was like a spider web of bridges, all connecting to make traversing the high houses easy.

They spent the remainder of the morning and most of the afternoon checking out all the rope bridges and treehouses for stability, noting where repairs would need to be made. For the most part, the majority of the system was intact. There was even an aqueduct system that brought water from a nearby river up to the treetops. The water, Silus stated, had once also been used to feed a tree-house nursery for growing plants for food.

The hour was growing late, and Harper needed to get home for Adda, so they left the area, walked out through the woods instead of taking the dark underground passage, and exited the forest where the road ended at the forest tree line.

"Thanks, Silus. That was truly an adventure." Harper smiled up at the large man.

"Sure, anytime. I just hope we won't be needing that tree-house village in the future."

Harper sighed heavily, "Well, we'll see what the council members and governors have to say in the meeting tomorrow. But, if my gut tells me anything, we may need it sooner than later. I know Raif Martray, and war is imminent."

"Well, good luck with that. I'll be waiting to hear from you all on what was discussed."

With that, they all parted ways.

Harper and Wilkins headed home, picking up Adda from Gracelynn on the way. Nan Trea agreed to watch Adda the next morning so that Harper could attend the meeting in Martanzia, but from a safe distance. She did *not* want to run into Raif Martray, but she *did* want to attend the governor's council meeting. Perhaps she and Wilkins could use an Image Enhancer to change their appearances, and she could wear a long robe to hide her body type and tale-tale habitual movements. That should keep Martray from locating her. But the real question was, would she be able to control her own emotions should she run into the man?

The Martanzia City Hall building was bustling with activity the next morning. They had decided to use MADs to travel that morning, not wishing to chance missing something important by being late. Aaric had finally heard from the Governor of Loradin yesterday about today's meeting and was asked to come along. He still would have attended even if his presence hadn't been requested. He took matters of the governments to be of the utmost importance.

The meeting hall was full of city governors, mayors, and council members from every large city to every small outlying village or town in Zanchier. Harper recognized many faces from her three years running from town to town. She also recognized many of the Zanchieths from years as a debutante while living in her father and mother's house. Fortunately for them, hers and Wilkins' disguises were working because no one paid them any mind. They looked as though they were from the Bakrisian dignitaries. They were dressed in deep-colored, thin, flowing robes with large hoods and long, billowing sleeves. Their skin was painted in swirls of lavender and deep purple, with thick bands of gold and jewels hanging from their necks, ears, wrists, and ankles. Harper thought the gaudy appearance was too much and would attract attention, but Aaric and Kamsten had assured her that sticking out in plain sight was the best form of hiding. Martray would never expect her to be so bold. Plus, they had the Image Enhancers and looked nothing like themselves.

SG Boudreaux

As they walked the aisles of the slanted forum, they were guided to the front and lowest area where the meeting would take place. The higher parts of the forum would hear the meeting through speakers that were placed throughout the seating areas. Aaric was seated a few rows away so that they wouldn't be linked as being together. Not that anyone, besides Raif Martray, knew about the Image Enhancers, and she wasn't positive that he had figured that out. Kamsten had installed a fail-safe into the technology for the wrist device. If the device is meddled with in an unusual way, such as someone trying to take it apart to study the technology, it will self-destruct and send out a signal that it had been destroyed.

The meeting was about to begin as the last of the dignitaries were seated and the lead council member called the meeting to order. Head member and representative of Martanzia, Leon Presterwick, pounded the gavel to bring order to the forum. A hush fell over the crowds beginning with the lowest seats and emulated upward until nary a sound was heard in the large, half-circular room.

As he nervously opened the floor with the reasons for the meeting, Harper used her eyes to scan the room, searching for Raif Martray. If she knew him, he would be close to the council members seating area, his hand firmly locked around the throats of those he controlled. She wanted to see just how far his reach stretched and who was in his pockets. It didn't take long to spot him seated just behind the center council members. Harper's stomach did flips, nearly making her nauseous.

Her sudden discomfort captured Wilkins attention and he followed her gaze to see who or what was the cause. His eyes landed on Raif Martray who sat piously behind the head council's seats. An underlying smirk sat upon his features. Others might mistake it for concern over the impending wars, but they at the LSS knew otherwise. If it weren't for Harper's being present, he would catch him later after the meeting, snatch the man up by the shirt collar, and pound the life out of him. But he wouldn't chance Harper being spotted or caught.

Zanchier Book 2: Uprising

It didn't take long for tempers to flare and tensions to escalate about the wars, mining rights, and who thought they were right. The entire room was in an uproar as each mayor, governor, and representative of every village was trying to decide who they should form an alliance with. Each large city or territory had their own army which consisted of the Bakrashan Brigade, the Martanzia Militia, The Carpasian Marksmen and the Loradin Water and Air-patrol. Within each of these larger territories, each smaller city and village also had their own soldiers. Most allied with their larger adjoining city or counterpart. But there were a few villages that were far enough away from the larger cities, who knew they must ally with a larger force to protect their villages, no matter how remote they were. Then of course you had the cities that refused to get involved at all, claiming amnesty and self-preservation. They decided to refrain from the war all together, claiming their cities would be unaffected due to their geological placement.

Aaric stepped up to speak, calling for a check within the system.

"Representative Presterwick, I must speak on behalf of the Loradin Secret Society to alert the council of heinous and deplorable crimes against all people of Zanchier. The Loradin government has been monitoring the actions of someone in this room for the last seven years and we have sufficient evidence of many crimes."

Presterwick looked nervous, clearing his throat as Raif Martray sat up straighter, peering at Aaric Brinley. "You may speak, Mr. Brinley, but be very careful of what you say and who you accuse."

Aaric sighed, knowing that this would create a major rift. "It has been made clear to me by the very organization that I oversee, that Commander Raif Martray, the very man seated directly behind the high council representatives, has unleashed a weapon upon the countryside of Carpasia that has opened a void of tornadic winds that are deadly and uncontrollable."

The room erupted with those who supported his claims and those that denied his claims, bickering loudly with one another. "Furthermore," Aaric spoke as loudly as possible, "he has infiltrated the council and has bought the loyalty and sympathies of many members of the council, and we believe him to be the leader of the band of cutthroat outlaws known as the Scaithers!"

Presterwick stretched the neck of his shirt collar nervously as he banged the gavel loudly on the desk to try to gather some sort of control.

"Order! Order!!" Presterwick yelled, as Raif Martray stood up against his accusers, his hands raised to quiet the room.

"Where is your proof to such accusations?" Raif challenged Aaric.

"We have plenty back at the LSS. I even brought some with me," Aaric said, laying a stack of papers in front of him.

"What do papers prove? They can be fabricated. And what about this weapon you say that I let loose on Zanchier. *I* built no such weapon. If my memory serves me correctly, it was built by a group of ten scientists, one of which was your daughter-in-law."

The room erupted again. Aaric yelled as loudly as he could, "Under extreme duress and threats by you, Raif Martray."

Presterwick loudly pounded the gavel again, addressing Aaric. "Where are your witnesses? Produce someone who is willing to testify to this. I personally know commander Raif Martray to be an honest and caring man who is true to his word. He is for the people of Zanchier, not against them. You should be careful what accusations you bring against this man, Mr. Brinley. It is obvious to me that the Loradin government is not in alliance with the Martanzian government. How dare you sir bring accusations of treachery and treason against any member of the high council."

Harper looked at Wilkins and turned off the IE on her wrist. She now looked like herself. He nodded, doing the same. As they both stood up, they let the hoods fall from their heads, revealing themselves to the room and to Raif.

"I am Harper Fenore Brinley. Daughter of Zanchieths Derek and Gracelynn Fenore and I attest to the truths of what Aaric Brinley has stated. Raif Martray kidnapped my husband and myself, stripping me away from my children and holding me prisoner for two years against my will, forcing me to build the weapon in question. He threatened not only myself but everyone I loved. Not only did he commit these crimes against me but held many other people against their will in Vasalage Prison in the Northern Carpasian mountains. I was present when Raif Martray himself fired the weapon that created the void in space the LSS now refers to as the Dustbowl."

"I can attest to the truth of the tornadoes being formed not five months back," a man yelled from another part of the room. "I am, Rodan Tixtel, village elder from Sandedge Village. We are frightened that this tornadic area may one day extend into our borders. It is but five miles away. The small village that once existed there is no more. Many people lost their lives in the blink of an eye."

This made Harper's stomach turn, knowing she had helped to build the weapon in question. The room was in an uproar as people argued with one another. Council members argued amongst themselves, and fingers were pointed at Raif Martray and Leon Presterwick. Leon Presterwick yelled once again as he hammered the desk.

Raif stared down at Harper. "Yes, the daughter of the man sent to prison only recently for crimes against the people of Zanchier. Like father like daughter, I say."

Harper seethed, knowing that anything they said would fall on deaf ears. Raif had a lot of pull, much more than she did.

Aaric continued, "What about your dealings with Vonder Mortruff, Martray? Mortruff is the biggest crime boss in Zanchier. I have proof that Vonder does the bidding of Raif Martray, and both of these men lead and control the Scaithers."

People yelled all over the room, demanding answers from the council on these issues.

Presterwick struggled to control the room. "It is obvious to this council that no terms of agreement can be reached here today! In light of false accusations by the Loradin government and their allies, against the council members of Zanchier and Commander Raif Martray, we declare war against our enemies. Meeting adjourned!"

People yelled protests at the council's decision as they poured out of the building, all in an uproar to what was said.

Many leaders, mayors, and governors approached Aaric Brinley demanding to see the evidence. They also swarmed around Harper and Wilkins all asking questions at once. Aaric finally stepped up on top of one of the chairs to gather their attentions.

"Please, everyone, I know you have questions. If you will all contact the LSS building later this evening, we will join a conference call between all interested parties and take any and all questions then. We can't possibly get to all of them right now under the present circumstances. Since war has been declared against Loradin by Martanzia, we must vacate the city promptly. Thank you!"

Aaric stepped down from the chair as he, Wilkins, Harper, the Loradin governors, Praxtingen mayors, and all smaller village leaders banded together to exit the building. Once outside, they used the MADs to jump back into Loradin.

Aaric and the others stood outside the LSS building as they all discussed the mess that was now a reality. War was declared, and Loradin would now have to fight. He and the governing members adjourned inside the building as they discussed the best possible way to go about preparing for imminent war.

Chapter 15

Preparing for War

Loradin's alert system could be heard across the city and throughout Praxtingen and Carpasmere. With the return of the governors and leaders of Loradin and the surrounding areas, the city's emergency alarm systems began blaring all over the countryside. People hurried to gather necessary items. Those outside the Praxtingen and Loradin area poured into Loradin and its protective walls. Gracelynn and Neitha worked tirelessly to prepare the Loradin Theater to house as many refugees as possible, gathering donated materials from the local people and businesses. Nan Trea kept watch over little Adda and several of the other children whose parents were volunteering their help with preparing the large theater.

The LSS conference room and monitors were overrun with governors, mayors, town leaders, and certain Zanchieth council members. The LSS tech team had to quickly install more monitors so that everyone who had the ability to see and be seen could do so. Aaric sat at the end of the long table opposite all the large monitors. Each one filled with the faces of all those who joined the e-link for the meeting. There were at least forty people tuned in; some by speaker on a joined com-call due to lack of technology in their smaller villages and towns. The problem was, there were that many and more who were siding with Raif Martray. Aaric hoped to convince those attending this meeting to side with Loradin and the people of Zanchier.

The meeting was long and arduous. Some argument broke out over whether the LSS could be trusted since most of the leaders present had never even heard of the organization. Aaric had to explain that the LSS did stand for

Loradin Secret Society, and that the reason for this secrecy was so that they could infiltrate crooked organizations without being questioned. Now, the Loradin Secret Society was no longer a secret and he and his agents could be recognized, jeopardizing the success of future missions, and possibly making them targets. For this reason, Aaric made certain that the only people in the room were those who were necessary for the meeting. Harper and Wilkins were present of course, especially since they outed themselves at the council meeting. Finn also requested to be present, knowing Raif Martray better than most anyone else in the meeting.

Finn told the leaders all about his own past dealings with Raif Martray and the things he had been commanded to do. He also spoke of his own involuntary temporary involvement as a Scaither soldier, and how he only recently discovered that Martray had been the one to order his wife and children executed for his own insubordination. He explained how Martray had told him it was the government who had ordered this barbaric action.

One of the council members asked, "I've known Commander Martray for years now. It is hard to believe that he would be capable of such things."

Finn replied, "He's a con-man and a very good one at that. Trust me, I once pledged allegiance to the man until I saw how crooked he was."

Aaric replied, "The man has business dealings with one of the biggest criminals in Zanchier, Vonder Mortruff. How could you think him otherwise?"

"Raif always told us that he was trying to change Mortruff's ways of making deals. That Mortruff was a powerful ally."

"Yes, I'm certain he is, but do you really think that Martray is in business with Mortruff to try and change the way the man does business?" he asked, disbelieving the naivety of the council member.

"I've had no reason to doubt his honesty," the man replied defensively.

"Well, what do you say now that you've had a chance to view the evidence against him?"

"It is a decision that we council members will need to discuss amongst ourselves before deciding who to back in this war."

"Well just don't wait too long to decide. If I know Martray, he is already beginning to move against his enemies. I doubt we have even twenty-four hours to make ready our armies and to notify all the people of Zanchier of the imminent war. I suggest you all do just that, as soon as possible, so that the people may ready themselves and their families the best they can."

The Loradin governor, Jasper Jeffries, said, "Personally, Loradin will close its gates by this time tomorrow, after the outlying areas have been notified and people have been given the chance to enter the city's walls for protection."

One of the smaller town leaders spoke up over the com system. "We don't have that sort of protection. If our people wish to travel to Loradin will they be given sanctuary within Loradin's walls?"

"With all the outlying areas and the people whom we protect already, I am unsure if our city can handle too many more. Having said that, we will do our best to accommodate all who wish to seek sanctuary, but your people will need to get here before the gates close."

"Which will be when exactly?"

"By midnight tomorrow. You all have thirty-two hours to notify your people and give them time to travel here. Once the gates are on lock down, no one else will be allowed to enter the city."

Some began to protest, knowing that their people may not have time to travel that far.

Aaric called order to the meeting. "Use whatever means of transportation you have to move your people quickly. We cannot send out aid because our people need to prepare as well. Our military and Coastal guards will be stationed outside the walls within the outlying cities. Praxtingen will become the command center for the LSS headquarters, and any overflow of refugees can take shelter there as well. But we can't promise safety like inside the walls of Loradin. We have sanctuaries already in place for this, but we will not divulge this information at this time until we know for certain who is allying with us. We cannot give away any more information. You all have until nine in the morning to let us know of your decisions. This meeting is adjourned."

People began signing off and disappearing on the screens. Some pledging their allegiance to Loradin, and some still trying to argue their points that the war wasn't necessary, and that Martray couldn't be as crooked as his accusers had labeled him. Aaric had Kinley make note of all who already pledged their allegiances, and she once again clarified to those still arguing, that they must notify him by e-link by 9 am of their decisions. If he or Jasper Jeffries had not heard from them by then, he would take that to mean they were allying with Martanzia and Raif Martray. The LSS tech team was given the order to disconnect all e-links, both visible and by coms.

Aaric looked at his team of agents in the room. "We need to meet with all remaining staff and agents. Kinley, give the order over the intercom of an urgent meeting to take place here in the next thirty minutes."

"Yes Uncle, right away." Kinley stood and left the conference room to make the announcement from her desk outside of Aaric's office. Soon she could be heard throughout the LSS building over the intercom system. Aaric and the others with him decided to grab a sandwich and some beverages from the lunchroom area to tide them over. They had all missed the dinner hour due to the extreme situation of impending war and the meeting with all the other city ambassadors. Kinley had had the foresight to order refreshments to be delivered to the office.

"Bless Kinley for this," Wilkins stated, grabbing several sandwiches and a beverage.

"Yes," Aaric replied, "she's the best secretary I've had so far. She thinks of every little detail."

They sat quietly for the next fifteen minutes eating their food before having to return to the conference room. Once there, Aaric explained to the LSS teams and departments about the situation.

"Now, I suggest you all go home and try to get a good night's sleep and prepare your families for what's coming. It may be the last chance you get to sleep for a good while.

Everyone is required to come in to work tomorrow to receive placement orders. The tech department will be needed to keep the barrier up. Maubrey, you take a crew over to the Coastal Guard headquarters for that. But everyone, please take care of your own families first."

Everyone dispersed, as Aaric, Harper, Wilkins, and Bain, all went to the Loradin Theater to help Gracelynn and Neitha.

Bain stopped by LARS to check on Wynne, and com-called Seadon on the way. Seadon decided he would stay at the academy to help pilot the airships should they need them. Wynne explained that she too wanted to stay at LARS because of Roamey. Bain didn't relish telling his parents of their decisions.

Kreelie fidgeted a bit where he stood at ease in the line of new recruits at the Everly Sound Policing Authority.

"So, you're Kreelie Rintel?" Commander Raif Martray stopped in front of him. "I've heard good things about you. Like what an excellent marksman you are, and I understand that your talent deals with engines?"

"Yes Sir," he answered the powerful new Zanchier council member, and his new commander. His father had told him that Zanchier was to soon be under civil war. Martanzia would soon go to war with other areas of Zanchier. They weren't told which ones, only that they would all begin a quick combat course in the early morning hours before the sun even ascended into the sky. He and several other sharp shooters would take to the training fields and practice their marksmanship. Kreelie looked around at some of the kids they had chosen for such a task. Some were as young as twelve. Kreelie couldn't imagine them being trained to kill other people in a war, but he supposed that if they had the talent, then they needed every soldier they could get. Even if they hadn't even made puberty yet.

Kreelie himself, and one other guy his age, had been put in charge of the younger recruits. Why, he didn't know. He had never really dealt with younger kids before and wasn't even sure they would listen to him, but he would soon find out.

Martray said, "We expect big things from you Mr. Rintel. I'll be watching your career with interest. And, if you ever need anything, you can let Riglan Mortruff know or simply com-call me directly." Martray handed Kreelie a card with his direct number.

Kreelie wasn't certain he should take the card, but he reached up slowly and took it. He turned it over in his fingers and looked up at Martray. "Thank you, Sir. I'll keep that in mind."

"See that you do." Martray smiled at Kreelie then turned and left. All the other cadets watched Martray leave then looked at Kreelie questioningly.

"What are you all looking at?" Kreelie stated. "Back to the barracks, all of you. We have an early day tomorrow."

They all marched back to the barracks with Kreelie wondering why he was singled out by the commander. He was nothing special. No more than anyone else anyway. Kreelie shrugged it off and found his bunk to lie down, anxiousness over the war soon to break out. He wondered if Bain were doing the same. Was this war affecting them as well over in Loradin? He thought about com-calling him, but then decided against it. He didn't feel like getting into another conversation about moving to Loradin. Besides, it was too late anyway. He was in the Martanzian Militia now and he would have to serve his term. He closed his eyes, trying to quiet his mind to hopefully find sleep.

The Praxtingen Airship Academy was on high alert that evening. The teachers and students all running to organize the ships to ready them for battle. Loradin was the first city to finance the building of the airships. They hoped that they would have an advantage over the other cities that they were engaged against. Not really knowing for certain if the others had advanced in the building of airships as of yet.

Zanchier Book 2: Uprising

Captain Matthew took young Seadon and ten other students to the airstrip with him to quickly go over any necessary instructions on flying and operating the machines. They had about fifteen ships in their fleet, but not nearly enough pilots trained to fly them yet. Each ship required a pilot, co-pilot, and two other crew members. Captain Matt was hoping to use several of the younger more gifted students to fly the ships if needed. And Seadon Brinley was the brightest of all those at the academy.

As Captain Matt explained to the young trainees about what would be expected of them, he silently prayed that the Creator would deliver them all safely.

Patrice Barrister had been on the phone all evening with the parents of the LARS students. Many of the parents wanting to take their children home for protection. She assured them all that the safest place for the students was inside the Loradin city walls, and that she had another safe house in place should the institute fall under attack. Also, ever since the Kabihanxu flight within the city walls, the coastal guard and the LSS had been more interested in the happenings of LARS.

The employees of LARS all ran around the building gathering supplies for a central location at the academy, stockpiling what they thought they might need to survive should the war escalate, and they needed to go into hiding. The students were all outside tending to the needs of the animals.

The oldest boy, Jerod Narta, who would soon be graduating LARS academy would stay on as an employee of the institute. He stood outside talking to the other seven students about the impending war.

"Listen up everyone, we have a real chance to give Loradin a one up here over the other armies. We have the animals. Since Wynne rode the firebird a few days ago," he said nodding at her, "I decided to try to ride the Monshokto, and it actually let me ride him, and we've bonded tightly since that. It really got me thinking that we need to try to communicate with the creatures here at the institute more. The animals could really be beneficial to our cause."

Oudree, one of the older girls, spoke up. "Jerod, the only animals here large enough to ride are the Monshokto, Roamey, and the still injured Yarequu that was brought in earlier this week. The others are smaller animals."

"True, but each one has a unique gift or ability. The Trefell could be used to chew through things, and the other animals, well we've been studying what they are capable of. Perhaps there is a way to use them? We just need to think about what it is they do in nature."

The students all began brainstorming the other animals of Zanchier and those that were available to them at the present moment at LARS. They hatched a plan to use the beasts should the institute come under attack. They would use their gifts to help fight for Loradin.

Chapter 16

Choosing Sides

The city of Loradin began to fill with people as other villages, towns, and cities began pledging their allegiances to Loradin. By midnight, the city coastal guards and extra military personnel began checking refugees into the city and separating any and all who were willing to fight for Zanchier's future. Many were sent to the coastal guard's outlying stations and, if needed, trained quickly on fighting and shooting. They were given a blanket and pillow and instructed to find a place to sleep in the already overcrowded buildings. As each building filled, the recruits were sent on to the next outpost on the edges of the island since most attacks would take place somewhere off Everly Lake. The interesting thing was that many men, women, and young talents, all chose to fight. The Loradin governors were reluctant to use those who were so young, but many were persistent. Especially those whose talents lay within the military or communications systems. Those as young as thirteen were begging to serve somewhere, ready to take their place to fight for Zanchier's future, their future.

Captain James Donner of the coastal guard had contacted Aaric about this problem, and they decided to place the youngest in areas that would not put them in the line of fire, giving many, positions behind the scenes. They didn't want to risk losing an entire generation of Zanchier's population to this war.

The next morning, just past daybreak, the city's governor gave the order to raise the barrier wall around the island. As the alarms blared the warning for clearance, the barrier began to rise from the edges of the island. It was clear as glass, with an obvious sheen to those who were close to it, yet strong as steel. It slowly moved upward toward the heavens a hundred foot into the air. The only way past the glass wall was the coastal guard stations where an access point was given to each station for purposes of war and protection. They could raise and lower smaller doorways within the barrier from a place inside each station. The battle airships, those not being used at the Airship Academy for training, now being readied on the Loradin Airstrip tarmac were capable of navigating above the protective iridescent wall.

Those in Loradin leadership positions, having had a long night, took a few hours to catch up on some sleep, knowing what could be coming at any time.

The coastal guard and the LSS sent out scouts to watch for approaching armies.

Back at LARS, Wynne and Roamey decided to take an early morning flight; still partially hidden by darkness; to see if she could spot any approaching armies. They first flew out over the land toward Martanzia, not yet seeing anything an hour out, but upon returning, she did see a fleet of boats amassing on the lake in the distance just southwest of Martanzia below Port Proud.

"We must hurry back, Roamey, and warn the others." Wynne and Roamey flew as quickly as they could back to Loradin. Their heat signatures being picked up by the LSS equipment.

"Uncle," one of the technicians replied, "we have incoming by air, but only a single entity."

Aaric asked, "Is it an airship?"

"I don't believe so sir. It's not large enough for an airship."

"Use the high camera and see if you can get a visual."

"Yes Uncle."

A few seconds later a picture of Wynne and Roamey came into view.

Many in the control room began to gasp and chatter, all wondering who this girl was riding the Kabihanxu.

"Calm down everyone," Aaric replied amongst the noise. "It's only my granddaughter and her new friend. I'll go out and meet her at LARS to see what she's been up to. What do you estimate her ETA to be?"

"Thirty minutes or so, Sir."

"Good, I'll see you all in about an hour. Paisley is in charge should anything happen while I'm out."

Aaric left the LSS building and drove straight to LARS. He was waiting when Wynne and Roamey returned. The look on his face didn't appear to be one reflecting a pleasant visit. When Roamey landed, Wynne dismounted and Roamey walked back to his cage for food as Wynne faced her grandfather.

"Hello Grandfather. I didn't know you would be visiting today," she said in a chipper voice, a large smile plastered on her face.

"It wasn't planned. The reason I'm here is because our tracking systems saw an unidentified flying object in the skies near Loradin. Do you have any idea how dangerous it is for you to be out flying with that creature right now? Wynne, we are soon to be at war. You could have been shot out of the sky, by our own people no less."

"Sorry Grandfather. I just wanted to see where the other armies stood," Wynne argued apologetically.

"We have adults that are trained in that sort of thing to take care of that for us."

"True, but *I* don't know those adults."

"You, young lady, are far too curious for your own good," Aaric said chidingly.

"Roamey takes care of me," she said, smiling brightly at the large juvenile Kabihanxu which squawked and danced in his cage. "And he's virtually indestructible."

"Perhaps, but you aren't."

"I promise I'll be careful, Grandfather." She didn't tell him about the LARS students planning on fighting in the war to aid Loradin.

"All right. I won't tell your parents, this time."

Wynne smiled brightly up at him.

Aaric looked down at her. "How about a bite of Brunch? This may be the last time in a long while that the two of us get to spend together."

"That sounds wonderful. Oh, and by the way, there are an awful lot of ships on the lake pointed toward Loradin." She smiled again.

Aaric grinned at her and ruffled her hair. "Thanks."

They went to a local café not too far away from the institute. They didn't have much time to waste, but Aaric decided he was going to enjoy this little bit of time today with his oldest granddaughter before hell on Zanchier broke loose.

Bain helped pass out blankets and pillows and helped to get people situated until the early morning hours. He finally decided it was time to get a little sleep and eventually went back to his apartment. He crashed for about four hours, then got dressed and ate a little breakfast as he watched people hurriedly moving through the streets below his apartment window. He looked over toward LARS, curious about how Wynne and Raila were doing. He wished he would have taken the opportunity to ask Raila out at least once. He may never get the chance now. Would they even survive this war? If they did, would there be much of a future left for his generation? How many people would perish, and how much would be destroyed?

He sighed, finished eating, and put his dishes in the sink. He decided to try to reach Kreelie one more time before leaving for the LSS office. They were due back as soon as possible this morning. He took out his communicator and pushed in Kreelie's number.

"Kreelie here."

"Kreelie, man is it good to hear your voice," Bain said relieved.

"Bain, you too man. How are things over in Loradin?"

"About the same as it is there I suppose. Everyone is preparing for this war," Bain said, sadness in his voice.

"I wasn't sure Loradin was even involved in this mess."

"You didn't know that Martanzia declared war on Loradin?" Bain asked, surprised.

Kreelie was quiet for a few seconds. "No details were given, just conscription notices. So Loradin is who we are fighting?"

"Yeah, I guess, along with other cities I suppose. So you're involved with the military too?"

"Yeah Bain, same as you, apparently. I *do* work for my dad on the Policing Authority here. I'm actually in charge of the younger sure-shot recruits."

"I guess I just never thought that I would be fighting in a war, especially against you," Bain said, a numbness settling into his chest.

"Yeah, me neither. I guess maybe we shouldn't even be talking right now," Kreelie replied. "Sorry Bain, I have to go."

"Kreelie," Bain tried to call out to his life-long friend one last time but the line disconnected.

Bain shook his head, stuffed his communicator into its holder with agitation and left his apartment, slamming the door behind him in the process. His frustration and anger fueling his steps as he thought about how Kreelie had just ended the call. He was acting like Bain personally was enemy number one.

It was nearing the evening hour as the alarm system for Loradin began blaring once again to signal the closing of the city gates. The last of the refugees were ushered inside as the city began to shut up against impending invaders. The bulk of the military was stationed in and around the large warehouse type buildings near the Praxtingen marketplace near the entry road from the north.

Silus and several of the older, war-trained men reopened the Discovery Falls hidden communications room to prepare Loradin for untraceable communications capabilities. Many of the youngest citizens of Loradin and the surrounding villages and cities would work and serve beneath these men in that location, safely tucked away inside the falls' bunkers. Several of the refugee families of these children were also stationed there as well. Serving in whatever capacity that they could. Many of the talents of the adults being very useful. Some cooked, some cleaned, some organized, some planned strategies, while others worked on equipment updates and making things even better. A few of the men were even able to get the secret loading bay door to move much faster to allow for quicker escape from the enemy if needed.

The LSS had a skeleton crew that would operate the communications boards and work on technology that might aid them in the fight. Most of the LSS teams were moved outside the city walls into Praxtingen and at Discovery Falls. Aaric even went so far as to send several agents and soldiers to the Airship Academy to protect and aid the students and airmen who taught there. The academy had closed its doors to teaching but several students had no home to go to, so they remained at the academy. Many of the students in training pledged their services to the pilots of the airships. Some of the brighter students were given co-pilot positions in these dire times. Young Seadon Brinley was just such a person. He and nine of the other top flight-students were named co-captains at a brief ceremony put into place by Captain Matthew Easton and his second in command. The other pilots, co-pilots, and crew members, however few they were, now stationed at the Loradin airstrip would bring the battleships to the school to pick up their newest crew members. With the commissioning of the Airship Academy students, all airships would have full crews. At least two adults would be available on every airship. Each young co-captain would become the co-pilot for the newly appointed adult captains who once served as co-pilots, and the students would be split up amongst the airships.

With the sound of the Loradin alarm wailing in the distance, echoing off the surrounding mountainside, they all prepared for battle. Each team boarding their appointed ships to fly high over Loradin to go out and meet their enemies.

Captain Easton's voice could be heard on board every ship over the intercom as each person listened intently.

"Remember, each one of you has stepped into adulthood today. You are all now, and will from this day forth, forever be young men and women of the Loradin Airship Patrol Service. You've each earned your positions here today. Make Loradin proud, protect her citizens, and perform the duties given to you today with zeal and precision. May the Creator be with each and every ship and crew member."

With that, every member aboard every airship saluted the captain. The airships lifted into the air and began their climb into the sky as daylight began to wane and give way to a moonless night.

Harper kissed and hugged Adda, then handed her over to her mother Gracelynn. She and Wilkins left the Loradin Theater to meet up with Finn, Paisley, and Aaric at the warehouses near the Praxtingen Market. These warehouses gave them a large area to be able to monitor the main access point into the city.

When they arrived, they were greeted by a few other LSS agents appointed to locate and deliver them to Uncle, who was located on the upper most level of the building where one of the office rooms had been turned into a command center. From there, they could use the antiquated, yet still extremely viable communications system which was located throughout pivotal points within and around Praxtingen and Loradin. These same communications bunkers were also located in other underground areas across Zanchier, as located by a map found in Discovery Falls. The resistance decided that they would take full advantage of these bunkers so that they could spy and keep tabs on the enemy's armies. Several village leaders who pledged their loyalties to Loradin had taken responsibility for bunkers near to or reachable from their own villages. The resistance now had eyes nearly everywhere, and their communications between places could not be traced.

Wilkins walked into the command center room. "Father, any news on the other army?"

"Not yet. Not by land anyway. We do have reports of their making an advance by water."

"We already have ships or airships in place?" Wilkins asked confused.

"Not really," Aaric said, uncertain as to whether he wanted to inform them of Wynne's morning adventure. "We had an operative who happened to get a glance at ships coming this way around mid-morning. I'm certain they are amassing an armada to attack Loradin at all points. If they can get through any of the coastal guard stations, they could overtake the entire city."

Harper asked, "Shouldn't the majority of our forces be stationed at those points?"

"Well, there are many fighters already there. Most are the people of Zanchier who pledged to fight, but they are willing, and most are able warriors. A man defending his home can be as fierce a warrior as a trained mercenary."

Wilkins replied, "True. Besides, the coastal guard is a pretty large organization, and those men know their way around weapons and strategies. I know James Donner personally. We were at academy together, and even back then he was always the serious type with a propensity toward all things military. He's good at his job, which is probably the reason he made captain at such an early age."

As they discussed battle plans and the rest of the room made connections with the other bunkers hidden across Zanchier, reports began coming in of movement from the Martanzian ground army and fleet of ships that was beginning to make their way toward the Carpasian mountain range. The warning sound for imminent attack blared from the alarms once again as all of Carpasia's citizens began to hunker down in their hiding or their fighting positions, preparing for the quickly approaching fight.

Chapter 17

And So It Begins

"Private Rintel!" yelled one of the higher-ranking soldiers, "Load your company, now!"

"Yes Sir," Kreelie saluted. "All right boys, you heard the man. Load up on the large Mod over there." He pointed to a large transport vehicle.

Caislan Harrington, one of the younger twelve-year-old recruits asked, "Why don't they just give us MADS to use?"

The other recruit leader, Droden, replied in a mocking disbelieving voice, "The government don't have the amount of technology to be passin' out Matter Arranging Devices to everybody."

Delmar Bamerly, another twelve-year-old sure-shot soldier asked, "Can't they just give them to the leaders and all the transport Mods pass through?"

Kreelie answered him. "No. The MADS can only transport one person each. They haven't designed them to move really large things like transport Mods. So, we travel the old way."

Droden replied, "At least they aren't making us walk."

"Yeah, that's for sure." Kreelie nodded.

As the new recruits loaded into the large Mods to be taken to the war front, Kreelie's father, Durger, was frantically searching for him. He spotted Kreelie just as he was about to climb into the transport.

"Kreelie!" he yelled to get his attention.

Kreelie looked up to see his father pushing through the crowds of soldiers to get to him.

"I'll be right back," he said to Droden and the others. He met his father halfway.

"Son, am I glad I caught you."

"Why, Is something wrong, Father?"

Durger looked around to see who was within earshot. He lowered his voice so only Kreelie could hear him. "You need to be careful and watch your back. This war isn't all that it seems to be."

"What do you mean?" Kreelie asked confused.

Durger nervously looked around as some of the higher ups began to look their way. "I can't say much more, just, don't trust Martray. All right?"

"I don't understand, Father. Why shouldn't I trust him all of a sudden?"

"Just trust me, Kreelie. I'll explain more later when I can get a secure line to com-call you on. I've got to go, they are watching me, but I had to see you before you left. Be safe son. I love you."

"I love you too, Father," Kreelie replied, a bit confused. He watched his father nervously look around, and upon seeing some of Kreelie's commanders coming their way, quickly disappear into the crowd of soldiers.

The two higher ranking soldiers stopped in front of Kreelie. "Soldier, what was that man saying to you?"

"That man is my father. He was telling me goodbye and to be careful."

The soldiers exchanged looks. "Is that all he said?"

"He told me he loved me," Kreelie said with a shrug.

They both studied him for a moment. "All right. Go on about your business soldier."

Kreelie nodded at them, curiosity about their interest in his father now making him wonder what his father was talking about, and why he seemed so frightened. He climbed up into the transport and settled in for the ride, unsure exactly where they were going but assumed it was to Loradin; his unsettled mind now having one more thing to ponder.

In the Praxtingen and Loradin home-bases, reports were coming in on enemy movement from as far out as the lower regions of the Bakrashan territories near Reef Edge. The Xantifa Tribe, Terra Valley, and Treeline Valley on the western side of Everly Lake had pledged their allegiances to

Loradin, which was very beneficial because they had very skilled warriors and hunters within their own villages. The cities on the eastern side which also pledged to Loradin were Carpasmere, and Sand Edge Village. Rhamadon, a large city to the east on the edge of the sand would support no one. Their leaders also warned they would not hesitate to protect the city from anyone they deemed to be invaders.

The village leaders of Cedar Mills wanted to pledge to Loradin but being centrally located between the larger villages of Reef Edge and Cyprus Ridge made their decision for them; having to pledge to Martanzia or face complete annihilation. Bakrashan, Everly-Sound, and Port Proud all pledged to Martanzia along with the Scaithers. Any of the miners and field workers who were at mining camps and harvest homes, were conscripted into the war. Production in the mines and fields had ceased completely.

Overton Colony, a mid-sized city on the southernmost region of the Carpasian Mountains, and Wickstock, a larger city on the western region of the Bakrisian Mountains decided to stay neutral, citing that the war wouldn't reach into those regions of Zanchier. They were both peaceable cities that kept mainly to themselves. Their cities were both bordered by thick stone castle walls and all residents lived inside these walls. The fortresses were strategically placed within the thickest parts of the mountain chains. Both cities were completely self-reliant, this being what influenced their decision, thinking that this war would in no way affect their fair cities. However, these decisions would prove to be grievous oversights.

The only other citizens of Zanchier that did not belong to any city or village, and that kept to their own, were the gypsies. No one knew where they would be at any given time. They had their own ways of traveling and made their own rules for living. They bothered no one, went about their own business, and traded goods with whatever city or village where they found themselves. They practiced wild-crafting for herbs and made tinctures and medicines that were highly sought after. They too, would stay as far away from the warring cities as possible. However, to say the war would not affect the gypsies was incorrect. Most cities they traded with would be at war, so therefore bartering and sales would be halted for the foreseeable near future.

"Uncle," called an agent monitoring the screens.

"What is it?" Aaric asked, moving closer to the man.

"Operatives are reporting a large mass of transport modules moving this way out of Port Proud."

Aaric sighed heavily, "And so it begins. Wilkins, you, Finn, and Paisley, take your troops and wait at the border of the open market. There should be plenty of places there where you can set up as snipers. I don't like killing, but that's exactly what they are here to do to us. Be safe and may the Creator protect each and every one of you."

Harper grabbed a weapon and set out after them.

Wilkins stopped her.

"Harper, stay here."

"No, Wilkins, I will not stay here. Not when nearly everyone I know and love is in danger and fighting on the front lines."

"Harper, someone has to survive this war for our children."

"Then you best be as good a shot as I am, because I'm not losing you again either." She squared her shoulders and left by way of the stairs leading down to the bottom level.

Wilkins shook his head, knowing there was no way to talk her into staying behind.

Bain watched his parents leave, grabbed a gun, and followed them from further behind. He knew they would both balk at his fighting beside them. Besides, he was nowhere near as good a shot as either of his parents. They both had plenty of life experience in the fighting department. But he would not sit back in the safety of the command center and let his whole family fight alone, which brought his thoughts to Seadon and Wynne. He quickly prayed for their safety. He watched which direction his Uncle Finn and Aunt Paisley went and followed. He would stand a better chance at getting to fight with Finn than he would his parents.

When the troops reached the open-air market of Praxtingen, Bain was taken aback by how eerily quiet it was. He had never seen the market closed. It was usually bustling with activity and energy. Now, the stalls were all closed up and the streets silent. Not even a bird could be heard singing, as if they too knew what was coming. He found a place to hunker down beside Finn and Paisley, who both shot him a disapproving look. He simply shrugged his shoulders and focused on the task at hand. They were to pick off as many of the advancing soldiers as they could. Bain just wasn't sure who was to fire the first shot. He knew that he didn't want to be the one to do so. He'd leave that to the more seasoned soldiers. He began to get nervous, thinking about shooting people. Many whom he likely went to academy with, and some younger still. This isn't something he ever thought he would be doing, but he did choose to come out here, so he would have to buck up if he planned on being a field agent for the LSS. He just had to remember; they were all told to shoot to kill as well. This wasn't what his bright future was supposed to look like now that the entire country of Zanchier was at war.

How long would this war last? Would things ever get back to some semblance of normal? he wondered, trying to quiet all the thoughts bombarding him as he waited to fire his rifle.

As the large company of Martanzian soldiers traveled through Carpasmere, Kreelie and the others felt a sense of impending doom as they looked around at all the abandoned homes and businesses. Nothing stirred in the stillness. It felt eerie, creating a sadness in Kreelie, one he couldn't quite explain or understand. He just knew that things were about to change forever. Life would never be the same again.

The transports slowed to a stop, and this was their cue. Kreelie and the sharp-shooters quickly filed out of the transport and spanned out in the advancing direction. They would walk the remaining few miles, slinking forward from amongst the now abandoned homes and buildings. They would find a secure place in one of them or the surrounding hills and trees, getting close enough for their long-range weapons to reach their targets. Caislan and Delmar stuck close to Kreelie as usual. Back at training camp, they were bullied by Riglan, so Kreelie had taken them under his wing for protection, standing up to Riglan on their behalf. They now stuck to him like glue. Kreelie was okay with it though, the younger boys were pretty cool.

"Stay low and out of sight," Kreelie warned them. "They will have sharp-shooters as well."

Caislan and Delmar both looked at one another, a touch of fear in their eyes.

Kreelie watched the exchange. "If you get into trouble, then either run and hide or surrender. They won't likely kill you if they realize how young you are."

They both nodded their understanding, slowly raised the window of the building they were in and peered through their scopes as they rested their guns on the windowsill. They all three scanned the buildings and marketplace on the edge of Praxtingen.

The transports carrying the advancing ground soldiers continued on a bit further before they stopped and the ground troops began lining up, awaiting their orders to advance.

Kreelie and the other sharp-shooters waited and listened for the first sound of gunfire which would alert them when to start firing upon the enemy.

This word, enemy, didn't sit well with Kreelie. How did people just like them, suddenly become their enemy? Nothing had happened. There were no reports that he knew of where any town or city had been attacked or destroyed. The Martanzian government had just suddenly called a state of war against Loradin and half the country, and the citizens were all supposed to comply because they were instructed to do so. Young kids were conscripted into this war if those in charge deemed their talent to be of any use. He just couldn't shake the feeling that something wasn't right. His father had said just as much in the rather cryptic message just a few hours ago. He had brushed it off earlier, but now, as he looked at the younger boys lined up with guns ready to kill anything that moved, his doubts began to weigh heavily on his mind.

Zanchier Book 2: Uprising

Inside the Loradin walls the coastal guard alert systems were pinging as it tracked and monitored approaching ships from the north and northwest. Anyone hiding in any of the nearby buildings could hear the alarms.

The LARS building sat within a half a mile of one coastal guard station, and the students sat listening to the alert, curious as to its meaning.

Wynne stated amongst the chatter, "It's the alert warning of approaching war ships. I saw them amassing earlier this morning on the southern quadrant of Everly Sound."

"There are likely even more approaching from the west since most of the cities and villages likely pledged to Martanzia," Oudree stated.

Wynne said, "I believe that the southwestern cities pledged to Loradin. At least that is what my Grandfather told me this morning."

"How can we tell who we are fighting against? Especially since no one will know who we are," Naphin, one of the younger students, asked.

Jerod answered, "I don't know. So we will have to be extra careful when we are out fighting. There must be some way to tell which army is friendly."

Oudree nervously flinched. "I guess, whoever is firing at us is the enemy."

Wynne replied, "No one knows what we are planning. So, perhaps we should fly Loradin flags from our mounts or wear Loradin colors."

Jerod nodded. "Good idea Wynne. We can take the smaller flags from the front lawn that the institute has flying. Wynne, you take the younger kids and go grab those flags while we distract the adults," he instructed, motioning to himself, Oudree, and Matteo, the other older boy.

Wynne, Kasin, Jilly, Naphin, and Eckshum sneaked about the lawn snatching the small flags and poles from the ground, quickly wrapping them up to hide them from others. They ran to the back of the LARS building once more to meet up with the others. There were only five flags with poles, three of which went to those riding creatures, and the other two would be divided up between the others who would stay in groups.

As the students figured out a way to secure the flags to their mounts, the other older boy Matteo argued his point.

"I think that I should be the one to ride the Kabihanxu into battle. I'm older than Wynne is by two years. She's too little and has no fighting experience."

Jerod rolled his eyes. "Neither do you. You ever been in a war before now?" he questioned Matteo.

"No. But I am older and more experienced with my gift than Wynne."

"Matteo, she's the one who bonded with Roamey. If it weren't for Wynne none of us would have ever chanced riding the beasts. Besides, we need you to lead the ground team. The younger kids need someone older to guide them and make proper decisions."

"Fine," Matteo growled, agitated to be stuck with the younger kids.

Kasin, the thirteen-year-old girl, asked, "What about our parents? I mean, we are all from different cities across Zanchier. Some of us may be fighting against our own families."

Everyone looked around at one another.

Oudree said, "You have a good point. Maybe we should wait and see what happens before we just take off fighting. It would be really bad if we were to injure someone from our own families."

Jerod sighed, "You're right. Maybe we should rethink this situation. I know Wynne's parents are here in Loradin. Did anyone else's parents take refuge within Loradin?"

Only a few raised their hands.

Wynne said, "If I can contact my grandfather, maybe I can find out who we fight against before we decide to do anything."

"See if you can find out anything, Wynne," Jerod stated. "Let's all head inside before things escalate too much. Besides, I'm pretty sure Dr. Barrister will come looking for us soon. And knowing her, she'll figure out we are up to something so everyone play it cool around all the employees and adults, okay?"

The younger kids shook their heads in understanding, and then went inside the LARS building to hunker down like the rest of the citizens of Zanchier.

Chapter 18

Reactions and Consequences

Wilkins peered through the scope of his rifle, scanning the now empty houses that stretched along the road outside the Praxtingen city market.

His LSS issued earpiece allowed him to listen to reports from the command center to know what was happening, and where. He could hear his father Aaric sending troops out along the entire stretch of the water's edge of Praxtingen. Reports of large fleets of ships and boats were coming in. He even sent some troops to the bay just in case anyone slipped by to attack that area of the city. The coastal guard was protecting Loradin all around its borders. Plus, the shield that Loradin had raised earlier would protect the city as long as the defense system wasn't destroyed. Praxtingen had no such system, fortunately however, many of the city's people had volunteered to fight for what was theirs. He knew that if the loyal cities from the west could somehow reach Loradin, they might stand a good chance at winning this war. The Xantifa Tribe was a highly trained large village, whose men and women were skilled warriors, often having to fend off the Kabihanxus and Pagorinxes just to survive. Fortunately, they had gained one more ally. Wickstock, who had first decided to stay neutral, had suddenly changed their minds and pledged to Loradin.

Wilkins and most of the Loradin leaders had wished that Rhamadon had pledged to fight. It was a large eastern desert city and had highly trained warriors that would benefit them greatly, but they were staying neutral like Overton Colony.

Wilkins looked over at Harper. She was steady as could be. He was so surprised by her newfound grit at times he barely recognized her. Not that she had been weak or mousy when they were a proper family and the children were young, but she had been more passive and laid back. With what she had been through over the last five years, she was definitely more of a fighter now.

She turned to look at him and noticed him watching her. She gave him a half-crooked smile and her eyes softened to the point his heart almost stopped beating. He prayed silently that they would all make it through this. Their family had only just been reunited; he didn't want it to end now because of a mineral right's war. But for some reason, he didn't think that was what this war was all about. He figured it had more to do with Raif Martray and his hunger and greed for more power than any one man deserved to possess.

Bain looked through the scope of his rifle, watching and waiting, but not really knowing what to expect. He had never seen war and had never expected to. He realized that he would have to kill others or be killed himself. He thought about his family and friends, and quietly prayed they would be all right. He then thought of Kreelie. He knew that Kreelie would be somewhere fighting this war too. Bain just hoped that the two of them wouldn't cross one another's path. Bain could not and would not shoot his life-long, childhood friend; his very best friend.

As Bain peered through the scope he began to see soldiers from Martanzia running forward from between the empty houses. Suddenly, a shot rang out from the ground below. Shots began to rip through the air. The sound of gunfire was frighteningly loud and constant as people fell to the ground dead from both sides. The advancing LSS agents did have one advantage over the other army, the spy weapons afforded them by the LSS. The few on the front lines leading the advance had handguns in one hand and laser-firing weapons that strapped to the back of their hands in the other. They only had to make a fist and point the device at their enemy, pushing a small button with their thumbs. No one near them stood a chance. The only problem was that very few of the Loradin soldiers carried such a weapon. There had been no time to crank out enough for an entire army.

Bain sat back against the short wall of the roof top and took a deep breath to steady his nerves. He looked over at Finn and Paisley who were about twenty feet away from him on the same roof. He watched as they fired without flinching. He took another deep breath, then turned and engaged in battle. He tried to aim for older Martanzian soldiers as the Praxtingen troops ran out to meet the advancing army. He had to shut off his earpiece as reports from all over Praxtingen filled his head. He couldn't concentrate on the task at hand with all the distractions. Bain shot up a prayer, feeling odd in doing so as he struck down men on the battlefield, knowing there would be consequences.

Seadon stood by Captain Easton on board the battle airship called the *Celeste*. The sky around them was dotted with fourteen other ships that sailed beside them. As they flew over Everly Lake, reports of advancing troops were coming in over the radio frequency they were able to tap into from all over Zanchier. Reports of fighting on the western side of Zanchier had started about an hour ago between the Xantifa Tribe and Treeline Valley, against Cyprus Ridge and Reef Edge. Many ships and boats were also reported being seen on the lake, as well as on land, but no one had yet to report seeing anything by air. The airships floated over the water far below, soon spying a fleet of sailing ships on the water about twenty miles out from Loradin's coast.

"Perhaps the enemy has no airships?" Seadon said to Captain Easton.

"They are there boy. We just don't know from which direction they'll be flying. Best to keep your eyes and ears peeled. Make sure the Watcher is on the spy scope. We don't want any surprises."

Seadon saluted. "Yes sir, Captain. Right away Sir." Seadon ran to the spiral staircase in the ships center that led to the observation deck above, to give the Watcher the captain's orders. Orders also went out over the communications grid between airships of the captain's express order.

SG Boudreaux

The LARS students quietly sat with the teachers and staff listening to reports over the old radio the coastal guard captain, James Donner, had given to Dr. Barrister. As they sat quietly, they could hear the newscasters calling out that fighting had started at the northern Praxtingen road.

Wynne knew that this was likely where her parents and grandfather were fighting. The LSS would take the first line of defense on the outskirts of town since the coastal guard was busy with protecting the city of Loradin and its people, along with droves of refugees from many other allying cities all over Zanchier.

Dr. Barrister had told them that the only reason LARS wasn't asked to house refugees was because of the animals they kept at the institute. The authorities figured it would be too dangerous to allow regular people around the animals. The last thing they needed was an all-out panic *within* the Loradin walls.

They all sat and listened intently to the reports coming from the small radio.

Suddenly, Wynne could hear loud booms which sounded very close. She sat quietly, barely breathing, listening intently for the sound. When she heard it again, this time she wasn't alone. Jerod and several of the other students all exchanged looks with each other.

Wynne stood up and left the room as Dr. Barrister's attention was on the radio. She went to look out one of the windows that overlooked Everly Lake. While she stood there gazing out over the water, cannon fire struck the barrier shield that protected Loradin. The force of the impact made Wynne jump. It did not break through the shield, but someone was certainly trying to do so. She stood there watching as coastal guard boats could be seen racing through the waters of the lake in the direction the blasts were coming from. Four large boats went out across the water at breakneck speed. Suddenly, one of the boats was struck by a laser cannon, causing debris from the boat to fly out across the water.

Wynne threw her hands to her mouth, frightened for the men on that boat. She had to do something. Perhaps some of them had survived. She looked back at the room where everyone else was waiting, locking eyes with Jerod who watched her movements. When he saw her reaction to something outside the windows, he slunk out to see what it was that she had seen, as she left the second story floor of the LARS building. Wynne ran outside to Roamey, followed closely by Jerod who ran to the Monshokto. She and Roamey took flight as more blasts flew toward the barrier's surface. They flew up and over the barrier's high boundary, out toward the now splintered and quickly sinking vessel to search for survivors.

Jerod and Moshi, the Monshokto, dove beneath the barrier through the water; Moshi's protective barrier encompassing Jerod; to aid Wynne and Roamey with the rescue attempt. The barrage of cannon fire had stopped, Wynne assumed, due to the Coastal Guard boats that had taken to the water in the direction of the firing. She and Roamey scanned the water for any signs of life. There were a few men still alive, but they were more afraid of the firebird than they were of drowning.

Wynne called down to them from Roamey's back, "Please, don't be afraid. Roamey won't harm you. We're here to help." One man who was unharmed began pulling the badly injured men from the water and dragging them over toward Wynne and Roamey.

Wynne called to her friend, "All right, Roamey, you know what to do."

Roamey stretched out his four legs, clasping a man in each clawed foot.

The lucid men on board watched in amazement of the young girl who controlled the deadly bird. At that moment, a wake of water pushed toward them as Jerod arrived on the back of the large Monshokto, waving at the men to throw some of the injured across the large hairy creature's back.

Jerod yelled, "You'll have to ride with them to make certain they don't slide into the water. I might could handle one of the injured, but I don't think I could hold all of them."

"I'll ride. At least this thing seems safer than the firebird," one guardsman replied.

"I'll stay here with the last two men and wait for the girl and bird to return."

Back at LARS, Dr. Barrister turned to the room full of people noticing that two were missing.

"Where have Wynne and Jerrod gotten to?"

Eckshum raised his hand.

"Yes, Eckshum?" she asked the young boy.

"I saw them both run downstairs after the loud booming sounds."

Dr. Barrister stood and quickly moved, yelling to the kids, "All of you stay put." She hurriedly left the room and went outside to see if she could locate the kids.

Wynne, checking to see if their telepathic abilities would work with each other, telepathically called to Oudree as they flew back over the barrier and down to the landing, carrying the badly wounded men.

Oudree, sensing Wynne's call, ran outside to notify Dr. Barrister when they spotted Roamey with four men clutched within his massive claws.

Everyone was watching the scene below from the upstairs windows when Roamey landed, lying the injured men on the concrete slab near the back doors.

They all ran outside to help with the injured men. As they all reached the dock, Jerod and Moshi swam up to the docks with more injured.

Wynne looked at Jerod who telepathically communicated that there were three men still waiting on the sinking boat. Wynne and Roamey took off again, much to the aggravation and frantic calls of Dr. Barrister.

"Wynne! Stop!" But she knew her calls fell on deaf ears.

Wynne and Roamey returned to the boat as a boom was heard in the distance. Roamey carefully lifted the last two wounded men as the other climbed on the bird's back behind Wynne. Just when they lifted into the air, Roamey let out a loud squawk as he dodged a blast of cannon fire. A ship was sailing quickly toward them. Roamey flew toward the vessel and blew out a streak of molten fire that set the entire ship ablaze.

"All right, Roamey, that's enough, take the wounded men home," she called out loud.

She turned to the man behind her, "Should we pick up survivors?" she questioned him.

"No, the other Coastal guard boats will return soon enough and pluck them out of the water. Let them sit there for a while."

They continued on to LARS, and once they had landed Dr. Barrister began to chide Wynne and Jerod for their actions, as the soldiers were tended by the others.

"What do you two think you were doing?" she yelled angrily. "You both could have been killed!"

"Yes ma'am, but..." Jerod pleaded.

"At..." she warned him, holding her hand up to silence him.

"You are both children. Not soldiers. I cannot believe that you would do such a thing."

"Ma'am," the man who rode aback Roamey with Wynne spoke up. "May I say something?"

She turned to him, fuming mad, but shook her head in allowance.

"I understand they are young and that it could have been dangerous, but if it hadn't had been for these two very brave, and obviously very unique young people, me and my men would have drowned. We owe them our lives, hoping that is, that all my men are all right. I don't know what you are teaching these children here, but you are doing an amazing job of it. I and the others were all shocked and amazed to see the girl and boy riding in cooperation with the beasts."

Wynne and Jerod looked at each other and smiled, but the smile soon went away when they saw that Dr. Barrister's attention had returned to them.

Wynne stepped forward, "May I speak ma'am?" she asked.

Dr. Barrister breathed deeply and nodded her acceptance.

"When I heard the cannon fire hitting the barrier right outside our doors I went to look. I saw the boats leave in pursuit and then the boat got struck. I just reacted. I couldn't just leave them out in the water to die. I had to see if any were alive."

Jerod stepped up beside her. "And I had to help her. What's the point of our abilities if we can't use them to help others?"

Dr. Barrister seemed to calm down as she turned to look back at the injured still lying about on the ground. Sounds of cannon fire could still be heard across the lake.

"Come on you two, let's see about getting these men inside to safety where we can better tend their wounds. But this conversation is far from over. We will discuss your *over-reactions* and the coming consequences."

"Yes ma'am," they both said in unison, hoping she wouldn't literally ground them from the animals.

Back at Discovery Falls Silus was in communication with the leaders of the resistance fighting for Loradin, and they had already set a plan in motion and had headed out to implement that plan. He spoke with Aaric over the old communications line.

"There's a secret tunnel that leads to Fort Arvenguard. Rodan, the village leader from Sand Edge, and some of the Carpasmere leaders, have taken the tunnel to the fort. They mean to come in behind the Martanzian army. We can strike from both sides."

Aaric replied, "We aren't certain how large this army is. Tell them to be careful. The Martanzian army may have already occupied the fort."

"I don't see any reason for that," Silus stated. "There hasn't been anyone there for hundreds of years. Besides, the tunnels lead up to a secret entrance. About a fourth of their troops could get into battle position before they are even spotted."

"Good luck and a prayer to the Creator for safety. Uncle out."

On the northern road to Carpasmere, Rodan led a large group of battle-ready men and women who rapidly sneaked their way through the underground tunnels toward Fort Arvenguard. Their hope was to lead a sneak attack on the invaders from the rear. Fort Arvenguard rested between north Carpasmere and south of Port Proud in an unpopulated area. If fighting broke out, there would be no damage to any towns, and for this reason they hoped the fort would be empty and ready for use against Martanzia.

Chapter 19

Who's Fighting Who?

Rodan Tixtel led the way up and out of the tunnel that brought them through the mountains and hills of Carpasia, bringing them out at the base of the lighthouse which overlooked Everly Lake at Fort Arvenguard. Much of the army behind him would be able to fit beneath the structure in the large room that led out into the stone enclosed courtyard of the fort.

Rodan instructed those behind him to pass on the order for quiet just in case the fort was occupied by the enemy. He walked over to the large double doors, peering through a small crack to scan the courtyard.

To his dismay there were indeed soldiers set up inside the old fort, but he couldn't tell how many. Perhaps a hundred from what he could guess, making this battle a long and deadly fight to take control of the fort. At least they weren't outmatched too badly as far as numbers went, but the skill level of the enemy was still in question.

When the room beneath the lighthouse was full of his soldiers, they threw open the doors and ran out to fight, taking the enemy by surprise.

Rodan yelled as they ran, "For Mackaby and Sandedge!"

His warriors echoing his words in one large, unified chorus, "For Mackaby and Sandedge!"

Shots rang out as bullets flew by their heads from the ledges that ran along the top walls of the fort. Some were struck down as they fought for their lives. Some of the men who fired at them fell to their deaths as Rodan's soldiers returned fire. Two of the LSS agents who fought with Rodan wore hand lasers, striking down many of their enemies which gave his people an advantage in the fight. After fifteen minutes of heavy fighting, the remaining soldiers for

Martanzia surrendered their posts and threw down their weapons.

Rodan's troops cheered in their small victory, but now the daunting task of picking up the dead and burying them would take place. They would make the enemy do the digging and clearing for all those to be buried. The Loradin freedom fighters would take care of, and prayerfully bury their own fallen warriors.

Rodan radioed back to Uncle to inform him of their success and of the many losses in today's battle, which were recorded for the historical houses. After the graves were dug just outside the fort walls on the lake side, the prisoners of war were then jailed inside the center watchtower of the fort.

"Rodan," one of the other leaders called, "what do we do now?"

"Line soldiers on top of the wall ledges. Three more in each corner tower facing northeast and south, a spy scope at the top of the lighthouse searching in the direction of the lake. Then, four men on each cannon. Load the cannons and make ready to open the cannon doors in the event of an attack. All others stand by and be ready to defend the fort. We must keep control of Fort Arvenguard to hold the enemy soldiers at bay before they can reach Carpasmere. If we can push the fight back toward Port Proud, then we can prevent our towns and cities from much damage."

"Yes sir," came his reply, and he turned to start barking orders.

Rodan shot up a prayer, "By the Creator, may we all survive and may this war end soon."

The fighting was still intense at the Praxtingen main entry point and market. Soldiers over ran the market streets and there was much gunfire and blood-shed.

Bain turned his focus toward the city streets now, picking off soldiers not wearing Loradin colors. Thank goodness Uncle had insisted that the men and women fighting wear Loradin colors or else Bain wouldn't have known who to fire at. He didn't know hardly any of the people in Loradin and Praxtingen, only a few from visiting the market over the last four months, and those he worked alongside every day. But those people were very few compared to the army fighting today.

Loradin military wore uniforms bearing the Loradin colors and insignia as well, so they were easy to see. The fighting seemed like it went on for hours, but in all likelihood it had only been forty minutes or so. Bain was afraid he would run out of ammunition and be a sitting duck before the last shot would be fired.

A few minutes later, the Martanzian soldiers seemed to be pulling back their advances. He wasn't sure why. Maybe they had more casualties than they had expected. It seemed the Loradian army had been able to hold the defenses at the market, but Bain didn't understand how by the amount of dead on the ground. Perhaps the enemy's casualties far outweighed their own.

Bain took a deep breath to steady his nerves. Seeing that many dead people was unnerving. He put his earpiece back in to listen to the newest reports on the war. New recruits were coming to take their places at the top walls of the market. He watched as Finn and Paisley, who stooped forward, move to go down to ground level. He thanked his replacement, wished him luck, and followed after them. They all congregated inside on the upper floors of the temporary headquarters. Wilkins and Harper saw Bain come into the room carrying a rifle and gave him a chastising look. He looked away as quickly as possible, knowing he would get an ear full very soon.

Aaric filled them all in on reports from other areas of Zanchier.

"Sandedge and Carpasmere have taken possession of Fort Arvenguard. Once we make certain that the Martanzian army has retreated we'll send our troops to Arvenguard to help hold our position there."

Finn stated, "Won't we run into the Martanzian forces? They can only pull back so far since our troops are also behind them."

"Yes, I'm counting on it. We can trap them and hopefully make them surrender. I don't wish for any more blood-shed."

"Me either," Wilkins stated. "I've already seen enough of that to last a lifetime."

Finn stated, "I hear you, brother."

Aaric continued. "There are also reports that Loradin's shield has taken some cannon fire, but it has held strong."

Wilkins asked, "Where exactly?"

"Near the south-western area mostly, but in other areas as well."

Harper inhaled sharply, "That's near LARS."

"True, but like I said, the shield held strongly. The shore guards raced out and disarmed the offending ships. But there are many more on the way, and from all directions. Once we gather a regiment to send out toward Fort Arvenguard, then the remaining troops, minus a small crew of sharp shooters, will pull back to defend the coastline of Praxtingen. The coastal guard and other fighters have seen to the bay area. Nothing should be able to break through the northern or southern area of the bay. Let's just hope that the troops fighting can all get a good night's rest tonight, that is, hoping that fighting won't resume until morning. As for the western region of Zanchier, The Xantifa Tribe, Terra Valley, and Treeline Valley have fought valiantly against Cyprus Ridge and Reef Edge but have suffered many losses. Wickstock ventured across the mountain toward Bakrashan and held them within their borders. General Nettles of Wickstock is sending any troops he can spare to rally our southern defenses and aid Xantifa and Treeline."

Finn nodded. "Some good reports for Loradin today."

"Yes," Aaric replied with a sigh, "but it is only day one. I wonder how long it will take to stabilize and take control of this war? We need to cut off the snake's head, and that means we need to capture Raif Martray and his affiliates."

Everyone shook their heads in agreement before departing. Fighting would likely start again soon, and they would be called back to the front.

Bain squared his shoulders as his mother and father approached. He held up his hands in defense and said, "I know what you're going to say. I'm sorry, but I will not sit by and watch everyone else fight while I do nothing."

Harper took a deep breath, looked at Wilkins and then at her son. "I understand how you feel. Just please promise me that you'll be cautious and not take any crazy chances."

Bain was surprised by her reply. "Yes ma'am, I promise."

The three of them locked arms and went in search of food and hopefully a few hours of reprieve.

Reports of another fleet of ships from the northwest were sailing toward Loradin, ready to strike at their enemy. Sailing through the moonless night, they marked their course for the northwestern shores of Loradin. As the ships approached within firing distance of the Loradin fleet, another body of ships were seen flooding the water to the east of them, but no one knew for whom they sailed.

One of the Bakrashan captains asked his second in command, "Do we know who this fleet belongs to? I've had no report of any allied ships coming into Loradin waters."

"I have no idea sir."

"Well find out. I don't desire to fire upon our allies."

"Yes Sir. Right away, Sir," the young ensign replied as he spent the next twenty minutes trying to hail the other ships on the water but received no response.

"They aren't replying to our calls, Sir, and according to radar, it appears they are repositioning their ships to fire upon us."

"Then blow them out of the water."

"Yes sir," came the young man's reply. "Destroyers, fire at will at opposing ships."

"Captain Merrick, I hear firing over the radio. It's coming from the direction which we are heading. Should we prepare to take on fire sir?"

"We're too far away from those ships to be able to receive fire. Could we have Loradin allies in the water?"

"Not that I've heard, Sir. Headquarters hasn't reported on any such ships."

"Keep our bearing north by northwest. Ready weapons and prepare to fire upon orders."

The Loradin fleet slowly sailed through the waters of Everly Lake, ready to engage in a fight. When they were within a quarter of a mile from the other two fleets of ships that were already engaged in battle, they held their position and watched the fight before them.

Captain Merrick asked, "Can you see the colors flying on the ships masts?"

"They are flying Bakrashan colors on the fleet to the west, and no colors on the fleet to the east. Who could they be, Sir?"

"They appear to be Port Proud ships, but I am truly uncertain. Make ready for firing on command. However, we may not need to engage if they finish each other off."

"What if the eastern ships are our allies, Sir?"

"Then they should have known to fly the Loradin colors if they had wished to seek aid and align themselves with us. Although I know we do not have allies in Port Proud. With this unusual development, I'm not completely certain as to who is fighting who in this war."

The fleet of Loradin ships watched from a safe distance as the two fleets destroyed one another. They would be ready to defend their shores from whoever the survivors of this battle were; if those survivors so choose to engage in another battle so soon.

Fighting had mostly stalled as troops on both sides fell back to regroup their forces. The sun dipped behind the mountains, and most of the land was quiet, but the Loradian government still expected a night attack by water. The enemy ships that had set out toward Loradin were still reported as advancing toward their borders. They were ready with their own fleet, perched a mile from the city's shoreline. The only problem was visibility. The city of Loradin was a much larger target than the enemy's ships, so they might have a hard time defending their borders at night.

The airship fleet sent back reports of lights on the water below only a few miles away from their own fleet of ships. And they themselves had yet to have visibility of the enemy's airship fleet. If they had to wait until morning to engage in battle, they would have to return to the Loradin airstrip to refuel.

Captain Easton decided to forge ahead toward Bakrashan. They could engage in battle against the fleet of ocean vessels that had deployed from enemy shores hours ago. The airships could easily fly under cover of night since they needed no lights to see ahead of them. They could easily destroy the ships in the water without them knowing they were even there.

"Captain Easton to fleet. I've had an idea," he called over communications, explaining his plan.

"Yes sir, Captain Easton, fleet following." Each vessel responded in kind and the airships turned toward the northwest. As they silently sailed over the water, lights could be seen on the surface below about a quarter of a mile away.

"Ready ship's cannons, and take aim within five-hundred feet," Captain Easton called, as each ship captain did the same. "Fire at will."

A few minutes later, the airship Celeste released the first cannon shot at the water below, striking a target, and causing an explosion as the ship blew apart.

The remaining ships began firing in front of them, hoping to hit anything. The airship fleet continued their barrage of fire, and the ships were bombarded by cannon fire from above, having no idea where the firing was coming from. They could not see their enemy or from what direction they were fired upon.

After ten minutes of near direct hits by the fleet of airships, the lake below was glowing with fire and the air filled with smoke. People jumped from the burning ships into the water, grabbing onto anything that would float. Captain Easton radioed to their armada on the water of the now destroyed enemy ships. The Loradin ships sailed toward the given coordinates to pick up survivors as prisoners of war.

"Let's turn around and head back to Loradin. That's one armada that won't be attacking our shores tonight," Captain Easton stated. He was weary and downtrodden from having to fire upon the enemy ships, but this was war. And in times of war, everything could be expected.

The Martanzian army hunkered down within the empty houses of Carpasmere. The tail end of their soldiers who were first to pass the northern road toward Port Proud reported gunfire from the north. The Loradin army had somehow taken control of Fort Arvenguard, and the remaining Martanzian soldiers who had survived the fight with Praxtingen were now penned down between their enemies.

Kreelie, Delmar, and Caislan, sat hunkered down with other soldiers in one of the homes. They shivered in the fall cold that set in every evening now, unable to build fires in the hearth due to alerting the enemy to where they were hold up. As it was, they could be descended upon at any time. The Loradin army knew they had them trapped, so they were basically biding their time before capturing them. They had no way of knowing if Martanzia was sending in an army to back them up. Their communications system had been taken out earlier with the death of the com-carrier. Even if Martanzia did send backups they would have to make it past Fort Arvenguard first. He doubted that Commander Raif Martray felt any devotion to any of his men and would dare to spare troops to save the few who remained from the first deployed regiment. Kreelie figured they were considered a forfeit, a casualty of war, and he was beginning to think that perhaps his father had been right. Perhaps the commander was not to be trusted.

Kreelie wondered what he was to do now. He had the younger boys to look after, not just himself. Delmar and Caislan stuck to him like glue. Kreelie couldn't make a move without them shadowing him. He needed to rest so he tried to quiet his mind and curled up against a wall, his weapon firmly clasped in his hands. Sleep would be fleeting, and he would try to make the most of it while he could. Commander Raif Martray may not consider his men important, but they would all stick together in this fight despite their rankings. Kreelie closed his eyes to rest, knowing the night watchmen would alert them to any movement.

"Commander Martray," a soldier said. "Reports from our armada out of Port Proud says they have taken on heavy gun and cannon fire from the western shores."

"What do you mean from the west?"

"It appears that a fleet of ships deployed from Bakrashan has fired on our ships. Both sides have had many casualties in both sunken ships and deaths."

"What idiot is deploying ships without my express command to do so?" Martray yelled. "Vonder, find out what is going on! Tell the governors from our allied cities to stand down until I give them notice!"

"Sure thing, Raif."

"Commander, Vonder, is how you will address me from now on," he sneered at the man.

Vonder looked at Raif, nodded with a smirk, and turned to leave the room to execute his given orders. But he would not stand for Martray's attitude. The man wouldn't be where he was if it had not been for his own organization and dealings. Martray had best watch his step. He may well be powerful now, but not more so than Vonder himself.

Chapter 20

Into Hiding

Fighting continued at the first break of dawn on all fronts. The Loradin ship fleet returned to their former bearings after picking up prisoners from the lake waters. The other two fleets had destroyed one another, and those ships that were left retreated. More ships were sent out to replace those destroyed.

The airship fleet returned to Loradin for refueling after their battle over the lake, then took to the air once again.

The Loradin army at Fort Arvenguard held their position from new troops who tried to invade into Carpasmere by way of the northern road. Rodan's warriors at Fort Arvenguard easily fended off new attackers with the many cannons in the fort. While all this took place, the Martanzian army between the fort and Praxtingen was still trapped.

To the west, Wickstock still held Bakrashan within their own borders, and the troops Wickstock had sent south to Treeline Valley to aid their allies in battle, had finally driven back troops from Reef Edge and Cyprus Ridge.

The Loradin sympathizers held defensively. They never led an advancing attack, and all the villages and cities knew the fighting was only stalled for now and that anyone could soon come under fire. Everyone prepared to do battle with the passing of each second.

This is the way it went for the next month. Small skirmishes would break out here and there. Ships were deployed against Loradin, and their walls received almost constant barrage both day and night from different directions, except the bay area.

The small band of Martanzian soldiers still trapped inside Carpasmere sat waiting. They knew they were no match for the Loradin army and would only perish should they try. They were all growing hungry and weak as scrounging for food amongst the quickly emptying houses was growing sparse having to divide it amongst the forty survivors. One evening while out searching for food, Young Caislan found their communications radio and was able to repair it.

"Caislan, can you relay a message to command that we are trapped here?" Kreelie asked.

"No. There isn't any way to make that work. The circuit board was damaged. We can only hear reports."

Delmar added, "Surely they'll send troops to come check on us?"

Kreelie looked at the boy. "Don't count on it. It's been a month already. A handful of soldiers aren't important to the war. I'm sure they haven't even given us a second thought."

Delmar asked expectantly, "What about the soldiers that got out a few weeks back? Do you think they got through the Loradin troops to get word to command that we are still alive?"

"I would think we would have heard from them by now. We can assume since no one has come to our aid that those men have been captured or killed by Loradin troops. Not to mention the fact that they haven't said anything about Carpasmere or us in any of the communications."

They all grimly returned their attentions back to the news coming from the radio, which reported that Martray had sent hundreds of men through the Carpasian Mountains toward Rhamadon to overtake the desert city, and force those within to fight for him. The city itself had many a skilled warrior, but their numbers were no match for Martray's militia.

"Rhamadon is due East of Carpasmere. Perhaps they'll come get us on their way to Praxtingen?" Caislan asked excitedly.

Droden replied snidely, "I doubt it. Commander Martray only cares about winning the war, not for those of us fighting it for him". They all continued to listen intently to the war reports.

Further south from Rhamadon, Sandedge Village reported to Uncle on the movement to the northeast and the fighting that could be heard coming from the northern desert city.

Rhamadon's governor had sent out a plea for help to Loradin after the attack on his city had started, but since their refusal to choose an alliance and join the fight a month back when the war had started, Loradin refused aid. Besides, they had no troops to spare for the city who had warned even them to steer clear of their borders. Uncle realized that Martanzia would soon invade from the mountains, so he deployed regiments to that section of Praxtingen.

Rodan was worried for his village and ordered his remaining people to Discovery Falls for sanctuary, knowing that the Martanzian army would soon fall upon Sandedge. He sent a few men to watch the city of Carpasmere and the troops who were trapped there. If those troops still thought the old fort to be populated by a large army, they would likely stay to the houses. He also left a small group of twenty men to hold Fort Arvenguard and the rest took the tunnels back toward the bunkers in the mountains. Perhaps a sneak attack on Martray's forces at Rhamadon would benefit Loradin? But they had to find where the army was stationed first. They may be able to send word to Uncle and troops could be dispersed to overtake his army before they reached Praxtingen.

With the growing population of refugees continually flowing into Discovery Falls, Silus chose to utilize Treetop Village.

He called everyone to attention. "All women, children, and the elderly and infirmed, follow me. We'll need at least twenty able-bodied men and women to keep watch there as well. The village is hidden and hopefully forgotten about, so you should all be safe as long as you keep watchful eyes and ears to the ground."

Hundreds of refugees followed Silus through the underground tunnels to the village in the treetops. Once everyone had been settled into the trees, and men and women were posted on guard and given instructions on village care, which took a full day, Silus returned to the Discovery Falls command center.

Across Loradin at the LARS institute, the coastal guard soldiers had taken up positions on the LARS premises to protect the students and creatures. Several of the guards had asked to be trained to interact with the animals and ride them into battle, but the creatures would not take to them. Only the students could ride them. Over the last three weeks, the leaders berated Dr. Barrister about allowing the kids to help with the fight, but she continued to deny them. She would not allow the children to risk their lives, even though the shield's defenses just outside the institute were beginning to weaken in a few areas from the intermittent cannon fire. They all watched the small cracks that began to grow daily, worried that the shield would soon fail and leave them all vulnerable. Wynne and the other students decided it was time to implement their plan to fight for Loradin, regardless of what Dr. Barrister instructed. They would bide their time and wait to see what opportunity would afford them.

In the northern part of the lake, the Loradin ship fleet was off fighting to hold their enemies at bay.

The coastal guard fought on the shoreline from the west and south.

The airship fleet had finally encountered a smaller number of enemy airships over the northwestern section of the lake. They had taken down these ships and made them retreat but had also suffered damage. No ships were lost, but no less than eight would need repaired, and quickly. The airships were taken to the airstrip within Loradin to do this as it was more protected than the mountain academy, which now stood between Martray's troops and Loradin.

The Loradin City Theater, which once housed refugees, had now been turned into an overflow for the hospital to house the many wounded and sick. The Praxtingen hospital also deferred its overflow to the large warehouses that sat on the bay, now used as triage areas.

In the west, there was much unrest amongst the governors of Bakrashan, Cyprus Ridge, and Reef Edge. Those leaders were not happy with Martray setting himself above their own leadership, and had secretly been meeting amongst themselves to overtake Martray's power and lead their own armies as they wished. Martray's control only extended to the Martanzian government, not their own.

Leon Presterwick and the other council members quarreled over this nearly every waking hour of every day. Many were beginning to see the extent of Martray's control over some of the lead council members and the more powerful people of Martanzia. They were rethinking their own roles in the war and who they supported.

Back at the Praxtingen northern border and market, Uncle, and an advance team, were going to take to the town of Carpasmere to ferret out the soldiers who were hold up there over the last month. They would take as many as they could as prisoners. He did not wish any to be killed.

Bain, Wilkins, Harper, Finn, Paisley, and another twenty LSS agents, plus another fifty military soldiers, took the northern road cautiously.

Wilkins asked, "How are we going to get into Carpasmere without getting shot. Those soldiers have been held up inside those homes for a month."

Finn offered, "Hopefully, they are out of ammunition."

"What if they aren't?" Wilkins replied.

"There must be a way to distract them while we advance?" Harper answered.

Bain smiled, "I think I know a way. I'll be right back," he said as he walked away to make a com-call to Wynne at LARS.

Wynne's com beeped alerting her to an incoming call. "Hello?" she answered cautiously.

"Wynne, it's Bain, we need your assistance. Do you think you and Roamey could get away for a bit? It may be dangerous though."

"Yes, I think so. Why?"

As Bain explained his plan, Wynne listened intently, informing him that she would bring others to help.

"Great," Bain answered. "See you in fifteen minutes, and Wynne, please be careful."

"We will Bain." Wynne went to grab the others who quietly plucked the other animals from their cages. The students who had no larger creature to ride, rode on the back of the

Firebird, Monshokto, and Yarequu with the others, holding their smaller creatures in their hands.

The Firebird flew out across Loradin toward the eastern gates. The Monshokto took to the water, putting up a protective air-shield around its riders as it ducked beneath the water's surface and swam below the barrier. It continued below the water's surface until it reached the safety of the bay. The Yarequu, ridden by Oudree and young Eckshum and his Trefell, and Naphin and the Tribhon, charged the now temporarily opened smaller gate within the large city gate. This smaller gate was opened daily to allow passage for troops and supplies across the glass bridge. The Raisedback Vindaper moved quickly upon its short legs, racing to keep up with the others. Men and women ran to get out of the path of the quickly moving animals, especially the ill-tempered Vindaper, yelling at the odd group of travelers to stop and come back.

The Monshokto climbed from the bay, shook its thick hairy coat free of excess water, and joined the Yarequu as they raced through the empty streets of Praxtingen, Wynne, Jilly, and Eckshum, flying overhead on Roamey. The few soldiers who saw them were shocked and dumbfounded at the scene. Never before had anyone witnessed riders aback Zanchier creatures. They weren't sure how to react, although some did try to stop them with yelling and the waving of their arms.

Fifteen minutes later, they came to a stop on the edge of the Praxtingen Market, just near where the soon advancing army was waiting.

Everyone was dumbstruck to see the creatures and their riders, but Harper and Wilkins were more shocked and confused to see Wynne.

Harper ran up and hugged the girl who had jumped from the back of the now very large firebird. It had grown quite a bit since the last time Harper and Wilkins had seen it. Wynne seemed a bit older as well.

"What are you doing here, Wynne? Why aren't you all back at the institute?" Harper questioned.

Bain stepped up. "That's my doing, Mother," he said. "We needed a distraction, and what better one than all the creatures here."

Zanchier Book 2: Uprising

Harper fumed, "Bain, are you crazy? How could you involve your little sister like this?"

"Mother," Wynne put in, "We've already saved a ship full of men outside the barrier near the institute. We have a unique opportunity to be of use in this war. One the other side doesn't have. This is what I was meant to do. Please let us help. What good are our gifts if we can't put them to good use?"

"Can't someone else ride these creatures? Some of the LSS agents perhaps?"

"No mother. We've tried with the coastal guard. The creatures don't respond to them the way they do for us. We'll be safe, I promise. Besides, who would be crazy enough to fire upon a Kabihanxu. I doubt the bullets they carry are large enough to break Roamey's hide."

"Maybe not his, but you aren't bullet proof, nor are your friends." Harper turned to Bain. "What exactly was your plan here?" she asked a bit harshly, aggravated at him.

Bain sheepishly grinned and explained what he figured would happen as a result of the animals descending upon the city of Carpasmere. After explaining and getting clearance to do so, they set their plan in motion as the Firebird flew high out over the city. It had grown so massive in size over the last month that Wynne and Kasin's legs barely hung over its side. The Monshokto lumbered quickly toward the city, its protective electrical shield wrapped around Jerod and Jilly. Oudree and Matteo rode aback the Yarequu, which sensing danger, camouflaged not only itself but its riders as well. The Vindaper scampered along quickly on its six legs behind the Yarequu. Eckshum and Naphin, the two youngest LARS students, stayed back at the market, their Trefell and Tribhon let loose. The Trefell rapidly rolled its way toward the smaller city in hot pursuit behind the other large animals, as the Tribhon ran quickly, leaping up and swinging from available tree branches.

The adults all watched, once again amazed at the abilities the creature's possessed. The Monshokto reached the edge of the housing development and stopped suddenly. It planted all four feet firmly and let out a bellow that shook the homes and rattled the windows of nearly every house. The windows of the closest homes shattered into tiny pieces.

Just at that time, Roamey squawked loudly as the trapped Martanzian soldiers began to scamper from their hiding places to see what was making all the noise. Small Trefells rolled past the confused soldiers knocking several to their knees, and Tribhons scampered up their pant legs stinging them with their tails, paralyzing them temporarily as they fell to the ground. The Raisedback Vindaper dipped its massive head and threw men into the air, its sharp tusks tearing at clothing and skin. While the commotion continued, the troops moved in to round up the fleeing soldiers. Roamey flew around the outskirts of the houses, laying a trail of fire to block their escape, as many who ran turned quickly and headed back the other way. As they dodged the houses and trees they ran into soldiers or agents from Praxtingen, throwing their hands up in surrender. As they were all rounded up by their captors, Bain and Kreelie came face to face with one another. Neither of them spoke a word. They just stood there and stared at one another. Caislan and Delmar began protesting and slinging their arms and feet in an attempt to be free. One of the soldiers threw them to the ground and Kreelie instantly intervened.

"Hey! They're just kids. Take it easy."

"Kids with guns," the soldier protested.

"And you don't have the same on your side?"

"Shut your mouth, punk, or I'll give..."

"That's enough,!" Harper yelled.

"They *are* children," she spat to the soldier.

She then turned to Kreelie. "Kreelie, I'm glad to see you're all right. And no, we do not put children on the front lines here in Loradin."

Kreelie motioned to the kids riding the creatures. "What are they, Midgets?"

Bain stifled a laugh. "They were last minute recruits."

"I can see why," Kreelie said, admiring their abilities to control the animals on whose backs they sat.

Finn spoke up, "Time to gather up the POWs and march them back to Praxtingen. How many soldiers were hunkered down here?" he asked Kreelie.

"Why should I tell you? You're the enemy."

Finn stepped up to Kreelie and peered down at the boy. "I'm not your enemy boy. Now, I'm going to ask you one more time, and depending on your answer, depends on how we handle the rest of this conversation."

Kreelie felt quite intimidated by the rather large man. He squirmed slightly under Finn's scrutiny. "Forty who made it to today, unless your men made that number smaller."

"No shots were fired to my knowledge," Finn replied. Looking around for clarity and any response otherwise from his soldiers.

"Forty it is." Finn looked at a soldier nearby. "Take a head count to be certain," he instructed the man.

A few minutes later the soldier replied, "All present and accounted for, Sir."

"All right, let's move it out. Standing out here probably isn't the best place to be with Martray's troops just east of here," Finn replied.

Kreelie was surprised by his statement. "How do you know that our troops are that close?"

"We know a lot, boy."

"Stop calling me boy. My name is Kreelie."

"I know who you are. You're Bain's best friend," Finn said, peering at the belligerent boy.

Kreelie looked at Finn with dislike. Then he peered at Bain, and then at Bain's parents. He then watched Wynne, the little girl he watched grow up, sitting atop the firebird as it and the other animals walked along the ground beside their captors. It was strange here in Loradin. Things were much different than they were in Port Proud. The soldiers who led Martray's armies were instructed to kill any enemies that crossed their paths. Not like these people who never fired the first shot at anyone today. If the situations were reversed, the Loradian soldiers would all be dead, per orders from command, even his friend Bain and his relatives.

The POWs were led inside Praxtingen and taken to a large warehouse where they would be confined to lock-down until the war was over. They were fed and given pillows and blankets and reading material for the duration.

SG Boudreaux

All the soldiers looked at one another, unsure what to make of such accommodating conditions. This they never expected. They had never even received such things from their own chain of command. Some of the people they encountered here gave them dirty looks, but the majority of those they came in contact with were of a friendly nature.

Bain stopped to speak to Kreelie before he left.

"Kreelie, I'm glad you're all right. I'll come visit as often as I can."

"You don't have to Bain. We are enemies after-all."

"No, Kreelie, we're not. I was never, nor will I ever be, your enemy. We both, all of us," he said gesturing to everyone, "just got caught on different sides of someone else's feud."

Kreelie watched Bain as he waved goodbye. All the prisoners within earshot of their conversation now had some food for thought, and many were inclined to Bain's point of view.

Chapter 21

A Small Victory

Bain visited Kreelie daily for the next several days and their relationship began to renew, even though Kreelie still fought against his feelings that they were supposed to be enemies. He held back on truly allowing their relationship to be as it had been before Bain left for Loradin. Bain could sense this but was unwilling to let their friendship fall away.

On the top floor of the building at the office headquarters, Aaric tended to the business of war as usual.

"Sir, Rhamadon is hailing us through communications. They've held the Martanzian army back for two days now. Rhamadon's leaders are begging for help. Should I relay our position on their request as non-compliant, Sir?"

Aaric thought about the situation. Fighting on the Praxtingen front had been at a standstill since Rodan's warriors had taken Fort Arvenguard. Much of the Martanzian army had been positioned at Rhamadon. Rodan and the majority of his fighters were also camped out around Rhamadon and reporting on the fighting there.

"Perhaps it would benefit us to send troops to aid Rhamadon. If we can stop our adversaries there, then perhaps we can prevent them from turning toward Praxtingen next. Alert the city's Leader's to hold their city for as long as possible. We will dispense troops to aid in the fight there within the day.

Aaric turned to another communication's operator. "Get on the radio to Captain Easton. I believe the airships will give us a great advantage in securing Rhamadon's borders," Aaric commanded.

"How so, Sir? They have limited precision on their firing capabilities. If they fire upon the city, could they not cause more damage to it and the people that live there?" the radio tech replied.

"Hmm...you may have a point. What do you suggest then?"

"Well, Sir, I know this suggestion comes with a personal cost, but, the LARS students and their creatures could be used much more efficiently, Sir."

Aaric looked at the young man, his thoughts heavy knowing he would be sending children into this battle. One of them his very own granddaughter, but the young man was correct. Even still, he could not stomach sending them into an area of heavy fighting. The clearing of the Carpasmere housing development, and the capture of the forty or so troops held up there had been a very different situation. And that had not been his idea then either. Still, the young communications tech did have a point. If only the creatures would allow trained soldiers to ride them, but from what Aaric understood they would not allow any such change.

"I'll speak with the other leaders and get their opinions on the subject." Aaric left in search of Harper, Wilkins, Bain, Finn, and Paisley. He knew Harper and Wilkins would likely protest heavily. He wanted to himself, but those kids and their gifts could be the answer to ending this war quickly. They were the one weapon and defense that no other city had. Aaric found them all in the barracks area resting for a bit. He explained the soldier's suggestion, and his plan, to much resistance from the others.

"Are you out of your mind!" Harper seethed.

"Right now, Harper, I'm just trying to end this fight before more innocent people die."

"At the expense of my daughter, and your granddaughter."

"Harper, understand that this is the last thing I wish to do. But those children could be the edge we need to win."

"What if they get hurt, Aaric?"

"Trust me, all of this has crossed my mind. But they have the benefit of anonymity. No one will suspect such a thing, and the animals, from what I have been told, protect their riders."

"Not all the creatures have protective defenses," Wilkins argued.

"We can send the airships in with them, as back up." They can protect them from the air. But we are trying to limit damage to the city and its people."

Finn asked, "Why are we even sending them aid? They chose neutrality in the war."

"True, but if we can defeat the Martanzian army at Rhamadon, then we could likely stop the fighting and end senseless killing. Martray is ruthless and will kill anyone and anything that stands in his way."

"Exactly!" Harper protested.

Finn looked at Aaric. "You really think that just after a month of war that we can end all the fighting?"

"Perhaps not all of it, but hopefully, the majority of it. I've gotten reports that much of the opposing cities and villages are now rethinking their positions in this war. They are seeing the cruelty of Raif Martray playing out with the abandoning of his troops and sacrificing the young to the war. Many are beginning to change sides and fight against him with their own troops."

"How do we know this is true? It could just be some elaborate scheme to get us to lower our defenses," Paisley stated.

"The western side of Zanchier has already started to report peaceful talks and a halt to the fighting between Cyprus Ridge, Reef Edge, and our allies in Xantifa, Terra, and Treeline. They report that Martray expects all the leaders to take orders from him only, and that the governors of those territories do not abide the things that Martray orders. They've witnessed the cruel and evil way his men handle POWs and the rest of the population in general. That whole region is now fighting alongside one another against what I believe to be nothing but Scaither troops coming out of Bakrashan and Martanzia. Some of the council members have even hailed me personally vowing to change sides."

Harper asked, "Do you really trust these reports, Aaric, or the council members?"

"Do we have any other choice? Our own allies and spies are reporting that this is the situation and that these governors are truthful. There is much unrest within the head council members. There is constant bickering over Martray's methods, and reports that they've even overthrown Presterwick's position as head council member. Especially since discovering that Martray has been lining his pockets for favors. And since Leon Presterwick was the one who declared war on Loradin then perhaps we can all come to an agreement to end it before it really even gets started. We've already had much death and injury. Many people's lives have changed forever in the last month."

Finn thought for a moment. "Do we have any clue as to where Raif Martray is at the moment?"

"There have been some reports of seeing him, but only briefly. He keeps to Martanzia mostly since that is where the bulk of his support comes from."

"Why don't we send in a special ops team to snag the man and put an end to it that way?"

"Excellent idea if you can find where he's hiding," Aaric replied.

"Let me get in touch with my resistance contacts up that way. If Martray is in Martanzia or near there, they'll find him."

"All right, Finn, but make haste. In the meantime, we must deal with the attacks on the eastern cities."

"Sir," the communications tech called to Aaric. "There are reports of invaders to our south. Overton Colony is hailing for support as well."

Aaric asked, "How did they reach Overton without our knowledge?"

"Reports say they came from Everly Lake by way of Sandbar Beach, Sir."

Aaric sighed heavily. "First we must deal with the attacks on Rhamadon. I'll call LARS for Rhamadon, and we will send the airships and some ground troops to Overton in the meantime. Once they've secured Overton, then we can turn them to Rhamadon."

Harper and Wilkins looked at one another, fearful for their daughter and the other students. But they both knew that Aaric was right, and if he didn't think that it would be of incredible use, he would not have suggested sending in the children and the creatures.

Bain watched the pained expressions of his parents. "Mother, Father, what if I rode with Wynne? The creatures don't respond to us, but they will allow us to ride passenger with their bond-partner."

"I don't relish you out there either, Bain," Harper replied.

"I know, but I am and will continue to fight regardless of the consequences. I'll protect Wynne and the others with everything that I have."

Wilkins replied, "All right, son. I understand. Just make sure you both come back."

"Yes sir," Bain said with conviction.

"Father," Wilkins said to Aaric, "Harper and I will also accompany the children to Rhamadon. If our kids are going into this fight, then we're going with them."

Aaric shook his head in acknowledgment and contacted Wynne to ask for the children's services. The children agreed and kept the call to action to themselves. They were to meet at the LSS headquarters in Praxtingen to receive orders and protectors. The airships were deployed to Overton, and three hundred Loradin troops were transported south as well. They would reach the borders of the city within the next few hours.

In the meantime, Finn had recently received reports that Martray was holed up in his offices in Port Proud. He had some large warehouses that he operated from on the waterfront very near to Everly Sound. Finn's contacts reported no troops on site, only Martray's personal henchmen and those that worked for Vonder Mortruff. Finn and Paisley took the special mission to find Martray and attempt to capture the man. They would use MADS for the mission as the quickest and stealthiest form of transportation. As the Loradin army geared up to defend its borders and aid the very cities who chose neutrality in the war, Finn, Paisley, and six other LSS agents donned their gear, turned on their MADS and reappeared on the outside of the cargo laden docks of Martray's warehouse in Port Proud. Trying to avoid being seen by the guards who were stationed outside the building, they quickly ducked behind some large crates which lined the docks.

Finn, Paisley, and the special ops team of LSS agents split into four groups of two, each group going in a separate direction. They scanned the warehouse for entry points and made their way inside, with each group taking out the guards at the building's exterior.

Finn and Paisley stealthily made their way inside the building, working their way up the stairway to the upper offices, figuring Martray's office to be on one of the upper floors. Each team took a separate floor of the warehouse, quietly taking out guards as they went. Finn and Paisley took the top floor of the building, moving as carefully and quickly as possible. They peered into the small glass windows, which were a feature in each door. They soon came to one door that did not have a small window. Finn watched for guards as Paisley attached a listening device to the outer side of the door. If anyone was inside, she would be able to hear them through the device. She listened intently, trying to make out how many people were in the room. She could hear at least four voices, and the sound of someone being beaten.

Finn looked at her questioningly as she held up four fingers to represent how many she thought to be on the other side. They silently relayed their location to the other agents, and what they were about to do.

He nodded to her, and they abruptly entered the room, quickly kicking the door in and startling those inside. The men inside tried to pull their weapons but were taken down quickly by Finn and Paisley's precision shooting. On the other side of a large desk, Raif Martray stood, his hands in the air. Vonder Mortruff stood next to a wall of liquor and had been in the process of pouring himself a drink. The two henchmen who Finn and Paisley had taken down had been in the process of beating one Castor Briggs to a bloody pulp. The man's wrists were tied to chains that dangled from the ceiling next to a corner wall. His limp body slumped over toward the floor, his arms the only thing supporting his weight.

Finn walked over to Castor to see if the man was still alive, his gunned trained on Martray.

Before Paisley could get off a shot, Vonder had pushed a button underneath the bar and disappeared through a secret door in the wall. As she ran after him, Martray moved to get his gun, but Finn quickly stopped him. Martray raised his hands up once again.

"Try it Martray. I'd like nothing more than to shoot you where you stand."

"Finn, such hostility, we used to be friends once," Martray chided.

"A mistake I won't make again," Finn replied.

"So, why don't you?"

"What?"

"Shoot me where I stand?"

"I don't believe in unnecessary killings anymore, Raif. I've changed."

"Such a pity," Martray mocked him. "You used to be ruthless, and loyal. However, I suppose it is typical of Vonder though, leaving me to fend for myself. There's just no loyalty anymore."

"Is your kind ever loyal to anyone but yourselves?" Finn asked.

"No. You always look out for number one. I did try to teach you that."

Finn ignored his words as he looked over toward Castor. Several of the LSS agents entered the room, two going through the opened passage after Vonder and Paisley.

Finn stated to the other two, "Keep your pistol on Martray while I examine Cass."

Hearing his own name, Castor wearily lifted his head up to see if his ears were mistaken.

"Mobley, here you are rescuin' me again. You're beginning to make a habit of this," Castor mumbled, relieved. He was barely able to make out Finn's face through his cut and bleeding swollen eyes.

"If you wouldn't get yourself into trouble all the time, I wouldn't have to," Finn stated, untying Castor's hands. Just at that moment the remainder of the LSS agents entered the room, several coming over to help Finn lift Castor to a somewhat standing position.

Two of the agents hefted Castor from the room, while Finn kept his pistol on Martray.

Finn looked at Martray. "Move it. And keep your hands where I can see them."

Martray walked from the room, through the warehouse, and out the front of the building. Paisley and the other two agents were outside searching the area for Vonder but had no luck in finding him.

Finn called to two of the agents. "One of you cuff this man."

As the agents holstered their weapons, Finn and Paisley began walking ahead of them toward Castor Briggs. They were all about to turn on their MADS to return to Loradin when Finn heard a skirmish behind him, and a shot fired. When he turned to look, he saw Martray pointing a gun at Paisley. Without thinking, he fired his pistol killing Martray instantly. Martray had knocked out one of the agents, snatched his gun, and had shot the other. The agent lay there bleeding, but he was not mortally wounded.

Finn turned quickly to look at Paisley who stood there unharmed and somewhat in shock. Finn pulled her into his arms barely able to let go. He was thankful that he had not had to witness her death as he had his first family. Commander Raif Martray would never harm another soul again. As for Vonder Mortruff, he was now on the LSS' list as the most wanted man in Zanchier. And Finn would make sure he was found. Getting Raif Martray was only a small victory. But it *was* a victory. Finn only wished that Martray could have stood trial for all of his crimes and spent the rest of his life paying for them.

They placed one of the extra Matter Arranger Devices they had brought for Martray on Castor, and they all returned to the LSS headquarters building in Loradin where Castor could receive medical attention.

The airships sailed through the sky toward Overton Colony and the ground troops zipped along the roads below in the transports. The reports regarding the attacks on Overton weren't from an immense group of fighters, but Overton was a peaceable colony and had no warriors to keep their city safe; only men with hunting rifles. Some were expert shots apparently, but there simply weren't enough of them to protect the entire city. Invaders were breaking through the city's walls with large battering rams hauled across the lake on large ships. By the time Praxtingen troops and airships arrived, part of the western wall of the city had collapsed and the people inside fought with whatever they had to fend off their attackers. Many lives had been lost, including women and children.

"Captain Easton, Sir," Seadon called out. "We're in firing range of the remnants of the army still outside the city walls."

"Fire at will," Easton called in answer. The long-range machine-type guns fired a series of bullets, taking out many of the opposing forces. Easton sent four of the airships to Sandbar Beach to take out the ships anchored in the water there, which were supplying the invaders with weapons and warriors.

Between the airships gunfire and the ground troops who rounded up any stragglers, they made decent work of wiping out the Overton Colony invasion. The ground troops stayed behind to aid those who were injured and helped to bury the dead as the airships then turned toward Rhamadon to aid in the fight which was already taking place there.

"Wynne, how do you hold on to Roamey while he's flying?" Bain yelled to his younger sister.

"I just grab a fistful of feathers and hope they all don't pluck out," she grinned.

They smiled at one another as they flew toward Rhamadon over the middle lower mountain range of Carpasia. The city would soon come into view, and they hoped that they could aid Rodan's soldiers who already had engaged in battle with the Martanzian army. Rhamadon had managed to hold the majority of the army outside its city walls, but the Martanzian army had managed to break through a few of the city gates to gain entry to the outer square. Most of Rhamadon's citizens were safely inside the inner courtyard while its many capable warriors fought in the outer courtyard against their foes.

Wynne's heart ached at what she witnessed below. The city of Rhamadon had sustained much damage to the outer courtyard, and many of the buildings on the inside courtyard where the people were hiding were on fire. She could hear crying and screams of terror over the din of gun and cannon fire.

She, Bain, and Roamey flew low over the ground on the outside edge of the city's tall walls as Roamey blew fire from his mouth, scorching any and all who were fighting to get inside the still unfelled walls. Men ran screaming as their skin burned. Others who saw the firebird ran for their lives to escape becoming the bird's dinner at any moment. They were confused by a firebird attack during a war. It wasn't like animals to attack during so much chaos, and one so far away from the Xantifal Mountains.

The Monshokto lumbered into the gates of the city bellowing its low vibrating song. Men dropped their weapons, hitting the ground in pain as their hands flew up over their ears. Once recovered, this gave the people of Rhamadon a few seconds to get the better of their enemies as they realized the creatures were being ridden and aiding them in the fight. The Trefells tumbled along behind Martanzian fighters, tripping and biting them with their sharp teeth, while the Yarequu with its camouflage abilities reared up and kicked at men sending them flying, totally unaware as to what had hit them. The Tribhons swung from trees and awning poles, slicing at the enemy with their long claws and stinging tails, wounding many. The Raisedback Vindaper ran and stabbed at men with its tusks, bowling them over with their strong wide bodies.

Wilkins rode with Jerod on Moshi, while Harper rode with Oudree on the Yarequu, protecting the riders from stray gunfire.

Wynne, Bain, and Roamey flew straight upward, turning and soaring back down toward the ground, sending men running and screaming for their lives. A few bullets whizzed by them, and Bain fired back at the men who shot at them. Roamey screeched loudly, sending flames forward from his mouth and streaks of lightning out and away from his body, striking men dead where they stood. This caused men to throw down their weapons and run for their lives in fear.

The Loradin airship fleet arrived shortly after, bombarding the ground troops that were trying to scale the walls of the city to the north. There was fighting, chaos, and death everywhere. Even Ash Mountain, a line of volcanic mountains to the east across the sea, erupted in protest to the fighting, sending smoke and fire into the air. The airships were glad of the western-born wind that blew the smoke out over the eastern mountains of the sea and not toward the land. Visibility would have been impossible otherwise and the airships might have crashed into the surrounding Carpasian mountains.

The fight lasted for a good thirty minutes with the creatures following the instructions of the children. The children in turn, if unsure, were given instructions on whom to attack by their military and LSS agent protectors. The people of Rhamadon dressed in particular styles of clothing and body markings, so distinguishing between the armies was not hard to do. All the combined efforts of the resistance eventually gave Loradin victory over the invading army.

After the long tiresome battle, the children and their riders and creatures returned to the LSS Praxtingen headquarters. After rest and refreshment, they returned the children to LARS, Harper and Wilkins keeping Wynne until the following morning for a long overdue family visit by the entire Brinley clan, especially in light of the fight they had all just been through. Even Seadon had been able to join in as the Celeste and other airships put down in Loradin for refueling and supplies and a much-needed rest by the crew members. Aaric had arranged for transport for Seadon and little Adda to be brought to Praxtingen headquarters. The Brinley clan all hunkered down for the night in the barracks, each one of them happy to be alive and well. Many families were reunited that night, but some would never be so again.

Chapter 22

An Uncertain Future

Over the next several days, leaders from all over Zanchier talked peace, pulling their armies back, and releasing POWs. Since Raif Martray was no longer in control, there were no marching orders being given. The corrupt council members were being dealt with by the other members, leaders, and representatives of all the villages, towns, and cities of Zanchier. Plans to rebuild were being discussed as the people cleaned up debris, fashioned head stones for those who were lost to the war and began to rebuild their lives.

The Loradin shield had taken a beating from cannon fire, shutting down at some point during the last days of fighting. It had left some areas of the city vulnerable, and some buildings had been hit, crumbling them partially to the ground. Gracelynn, Neitha, and Nan Trea, started organizations to help those who had been affected greatly by the war, and making certain everyone had somewhere to call home.

Treetop Village became a permanent home to many of those whose homes and livelihoods had been destroyed in the war, which included many from Carpasmere. They kept the location a secret as much as possible, hoping to avoid the ruthlessness of the Scaither's ever growing forces.

Scaithers still terrorized many places, having become a lawless band of renegades who thought of nothing but themselves and placed value on no one. Their numbers were great, and people still fought daily at whatever town or village they decided to plunder. Vonder Mortruff was now head of the crime syndicate, taking over many of Raif Martray's businesses and organizations, financing many of the Scaither operations and placing his son Riglan in a prime position to one day take over.

Kreelie and the other Martanzian soldiers returned to Martanzia and Port Proud. His father had come out of hiding but was still leery of most everyone, often mumbling about Vonder Mortruff coming after him next, in an almost crazed manner at times. Kreelie worried about him constantly and had taken over caring for his father. Kreelie was soon offered a position as an inspector in the Policing Authority for Port Proud due to his heroic war efforts and recovered POW status. He also took in the two orphaned boys, Delmar and Caislan, and asked for them to receive non-life-threatening positions in the Policing Authority, which was granted.

Kreelie and Bain's relationship was on the way to restoration now that Zanchier's war was over. Even still, there were battles almost daily between the people who fought to restore the peace and governments of Zanchier and the Scaither militia.

There were talks of restructuring the governments and labeling systems since nearly all had fallen apart, and the lower classes did not want to return to their meager earnings and poor working conditions. It was without a doubt that the new establishing government was expected to step up and take better care of all of its citizens, wealthy and poor alike. Especially since many of those who fought had become war heroes.

Dr. Barrister's work with LARS and the gifted children drew much recognition. Many of the government officials and other leaders wanted an animal army. Not only did Loradin and the resistance desire such a thing, but most of Zanchier had heard of their great feats and efforts and began testing the "untalented" people of Zanchier to see if they were among the gifted, hoping to form their own animal brigades. Dr. Barrister however stated that the purpose of the gifted was not to fight, but to learn to live and use the animals in everyday life, and to prevent the loss of human life and to coexist peacefully with the creatures of Zanchier. This did not sit well with many who decided that they should be trained for battle in the event of another war, but she refused to use the children and creatures in such a manner and therefore daily feared for the children's safety. They were watched closely and warned about becoming too friendly with outsiders, fearful that the power hungry and ruthless would use the children's gifts to their own benefit.

Although Dr. Barrister protested the children riding the creatures for military purposes, the children practiced with the animals all the same and learned as much as possible about the abilities of every animal that entered the LARS gates. They found there were many things not known about the creatures in the texts provided for learning, because no one had ever gotten close enough to observe them in all areas or witnessed their reactions under certain circumstances. Dr. Barrister was very excited over this new information, but also very nervous at the same time.

Because of the war, the gypsy people who traveled their own pathways around Zanchier visiting most cities, towns, and villages for trading purposes, often captured, and brought injured or orphaned animals by the LARS institute for rehabilitation. The gypsies kept to themselves mostly, camping in their own undisclosed and often hidden sites during travels, which made certain they steered clear of the Scaithers.

The LARS institute was becoming overrun with newly injured creatures, and they were given more land by the Loradin government to expand the institute with no shortage of funding, volunteers, and people seeking employment. There were almost constant interviews with children whose parents once thought them without talent, and now hoped that they had the gift of telepathy and animal communications. Harper, Wilkins, and Bain often helped out at LARS to ease the growing pains felt by the institutes rapidly expanding walls.

The Praxtingen Airship Academy also had a new barrage of young men and women who wished to become airship captains and learn to fly the floating ships across the Zanchier sky.

The Coastal Guards ranks also exploded with new recruits. People who once took their freedom for granted now signed up in droves to learn to fight and defend what was theirs for the future of their children and all that was good.

Loradin and Praxtingen still had strong protections in place to take care of their own, and many across Zanchier wanted to stay in Loradin partly for this reason, but also because of its unsurpassed beauty. The cities now had no choice but to relax their strict entrance requirements with so many refugees without homes. Those who had taken up sanctuary before the war started did not desire to return to their villages. Some of those who did decide to return home found their homes destroyed and their villages leveled. Instead of rebuilding they then made the journey back to Loradin and Praxtingen, hoping to become new citizens of the cities.

Castor Briggs was healing in the LSS hospital wing and had asked to join the LSS once he was fully recovered. Aaric told him that they would see if he had what it took, and whether or not they could put their trust in him. Betrayal was not easily dismissed.

Rodan Tixtel and his people returned to their desert village as no damage had been afflicted since the Martanzian army had been stopped at Rhamadon. His village also grew in recognition and popularity as they became known as strong fearless people. Many dubbed his village the Defenders of Arvenguard, knowing that their holding the fort had been a major turning point in the fight. And many a young man and woman who were now without homes came to Sandedge Village to live and learn with these legendary warriors.

On the western side of Zanchier, the villages which allied with Loradin still verbally battled with their neighbors and war enemies. They were accused daily of being turncoats by the lowly and uneducated people who knew only the lies the Scaithers spat as they invaded their villages. The Scaithers often spouted the greatness of Raif Martray and Vonder Mortruff as the liberators of the little man, the people once forced to work the Rhe Mines by their oppressors the Zanchieths. The rich and entitled people of Zanchier had abused their power for far too long. Because of the constant reminder of the oppression before the war, these people joined the Scaithers and their lawless way of life. Reformation for all of Zanchier may have been on the horizon, but it would come too late as many were tired of the daily struggles, now made worse by the selfish mining rights war. The Scaithers offered freedom to do as one pleased, and in a somewhat protected environment, as long as one was loyal.

Back at LARS, Bain walked around the grounds of the Institute which now had constant construction happening due to the population surge of both animals and humans. He spotted Raila working outside near one of the cages and walked over to speak with her.

"Raila," he hailed her.

"Good morning Bain." She smiled at him.

"I just wanted to ask you a question."

"Sure," she said, stopping what she was doing and turning toward him.

"I just never got a chance to ask you out before the war started. So, now I'd like to ask you to go out with me sometime."

Raila smiled broadly, "Sure. I'd like that."

Bain smiled broadly as well. "Great."

"When?" Raila smiled.

"Oh...um, how about this evening, after work."

"Sounds good. You can pick me up here, say around six?"

"Yeah, sounds good." Bain smiled. As he turned to leave, Raila caught his attention.

"And Bain?"

"Yeah," he said turning back to look at her.

"Bring your Bi-mod. I've been dying to ride that thing," she said with a broad smile and a giggle.

Bain laughed and nodded and waved to her as he left to see to some chores. He smiled the rest of the day thinking about his date that night.

Wilkins and Harper were happy to be home again. They took the day just to enjoy being together with Adda. They gave Nan Trea the day off and had a little picnic in the back yard enjoying the sparkling bay water. They sat on a blanket in the yard and watched Adda playing by the water's edge of the rocky shoreline.

Harper sighed deeply which drew Wilkins attention. He smiled at the peaceful expression on her face.

"What are thinking about," he asked her.

"You know very well what I'm thinking," she said with a grin.

"Tell me anyway." He smiled at her upturned face.

"The weight of it all is gone. We can finally breathe and live a normal life for a change. The children are all doing well. We all survived that horrid war, no matter how short it was. We can finally be a family. Even though the Scaithers are still a threat to everyone, it's not like our family is dealing with being hunted constantly. I haven't felt this much peace in over six years, Wil."

"I know. I feel it too. And no matter what the future throws at us, we have nothing to fear. We both have great jobs that we love, financial security, well-adjusted and happy kids, even with what they have all been through. We should thank your mother for the great job she did with raising them for the last five years. Although, I believe most of their strength comes from you and how you handled them as young children."

Harper smiled up at her husband. "You're right. I do need to officially thank Mother for all she's done. As far as the great job goes, I think I'm going to take a break from work for a while to be with Adda. I was working for the LSS mainly because of my fear of Raif and my need to somehow be in control. With that fear gone, I just want to be her mother. Oh, did you ever find out who the Loradin mole was that was working for Martray?"

"Unfortunately, no. The war overshadowed all that. I'll continue looking into it though now that things are back to normal."

Harper smiled. She could relax her constant state of worry now that Raif Martray was dead. She breathed easier knowing that he was gone and felt relief for the safety of her family. She rejoiced in knowing she could raise Adda without the constant fear he had brought into her life. They both watched Adda giggle at something at the water's edge. They stood to join her in her play, both contented with life at present.

Across town, Finn and Paisley also took a long morning together. Staying home, relaxing, and spending the pre-lunch hours just lazing around the house.

They chatted about their most recent mission to capture Raif Martray.

Finn was deep in thought for a moment when Paisley spoke. "I just wish Raif Martray could have stood trial and paid dearly for his crimes. He would have never gotten out of prison, his crimes being so great."

"Yes, I agree, and I didn't want to kill the man. But when I saw that laser pointed at you, I just reacted. I will always protect you, no matter the cost."

Zanchier Book 2: Uprising

Paisley gave him a crooked grin, "And I you, my love. I am grateful for your quick reflexes, although you know I can handle myself."

Finn laughed. "Will you not allow me *some* manly pride, woman? I know very well that you can handle things on your own. I'm just glad that you allow me to be there when you aren't able. I couldn't bear to lose you."

They kissed each other longingly, enjoying the last few minutes of their restful morning before needing to head to LSS headquarters.

At Praxtingen Airship Academy, crews worked diligently to prepare the grounds for a ceremony and celebration. All the new recruits of LAPS, Loradin Airship Patrol Services, were to be presented with jackets and ranking patches in a ceremony the next evening. The Loradin government was also to attend to present awards to the students of LARS as well for their bravery and willingness to aid in the war efforts. All family and friends had been invited to attend. The students all excitedly pitched in to help set up.

The next evening, as the large crowd of people sat expectantly waiting for the ceremony to start, Captain Easton stepped forward. He began, first welcoming the crowds of people who showed up to support the brave young men and women who had done their part and more in the war effort.

"Today, we honor the heroic efforts of the very young. Our future generations have proven that they have what it takes to take our places as strong and fearless leaders. To face an uncertain future with resolve, cunning, strength, and goodness of character. These young men and women not only took on adult roles and did what was necessary during the recent war, they did so with dignity, and will henceforth be known as members of Loradin Air Patrol Services."

The students all stood at attention in line facing the crowd of people in attendance. As Captain Easton called their names, they stepped forward, turned sharply right, and walked forward to be presented with their jacket and ranking. When it came time for Seadon to be presented, Captain Easton spoke again.

"I wish to say one thing about this last young man I am about to introduce you to. Never in all my years have I seen a boy whose abilities match his. He learns quickly, like he was born gifted for flying. He can operate any airship with ease, almost matching my own abilities. I present to you the bravest of us all, and a future captain of LAPS, I'd say sooner than even we know, Seadon Brinley."

Seadon stepped forth to receive his jacket. The crowd erupted in applause and a standing ovation. Whistles were heard throughout by Seadon's family and many of the LSS agents who were in attendance. Seadon's smile was nearly too large for his face to contain, finally receiving his heart's desire.

Next to speak was governor Jasper Jeffries of Loradin who stepped forth to present the awards for the LARS students.

"As you all now know, we recently discovered a group of extraordinary children. I guess I should also say, young men and women, for the tasks they took on not only showed an attitude of understanding and adult thinking, but of extreme bravery and courage unmatched by many of us. I dare say they selflessly, and without any military training, took on the roles of defenders, protectors, and warriors of Loradin. We wish to present each of these young people with an award, and a key to the city of Loradin. If it had not been for Dr. Patrice Barrister's program and keen insight to find these gifted children, we may have lost the fight and been unable to thwart the enemy at Rhamadon. I present these young men and women from eldest to youngest. And I want you to understand just how young that is."

The governor called each child by name, giving their age, parent's names, and what town, village, or city they hailed from. When Wynne's name was called, she received the same kind of applause and revelry that Seadon had. She giggled at all the attention. When the governor called the last two LARS students, eight-year-old Naphin and seven-year-old Eckshum, there were gasps of surprise and the entire crowd stood and cheered loudly for them. All the students both from the airship academy and LARS spent the remainder of the evening being congratulated and thanked by every person in attendance.

As Captain Easton had stated, the future of Zanchier was uncertain, but the defenders and heroes were plenty and mighty, and they would all be there to do their part for all the people of Zanchier.

About the Author

SG Boudreaux is a stay-at-home mom who has home-schooled her children for the last twenty years. Two have graduated, and her youngest is a seventeen-year-old, special-needs child. She and her husband of twenty-five years live in the country, in a small rural area, just outside of Lake Charles, Louisiana. She was born in West Virginia, lived in Florida for many years before moving to Louisiana with her mother and youngest sister. She married a local boy and has lived there ever since. She loves the culture, the people, the sense of community, and definitely the wonderful Cajun food. You can find out more about her and her books on her website at www.sgboudreaux.com

All of her previous books are clean-reading, fiction, fantasy, and time-travel.

You can write to her at the address in the front of the books.

Watch for the third book in the series *Zanchier* to be released early 2022.

Other Books by SG Boudreaux

CPSIA information can be obtained
at www.ICGtesting.com
Printed in the USA
LVHW112025160921
697990LV00001B/67